"FRANCIS, AS WE ALL KNOW, IS ONE OF THE BEST."
—*The New York Times*

"This taut and sophisticated thriller strikes the reader with all the shock and impact of a bonecrack."

—*Publishers Weekly*

"Further evidence that Dick Francis is one of the greatest living suspense writers."   —*CBS Radio*

"Keeps readers on the edge of their saddles."

—*The Washington Post*

Winner of the Mystery Writers of America Award for Best Novel of the Year, Dick Francis is the bestselling author of *Enquiry, Knockdown, For Kicks, Nerve, Forfeit, Dead Cert, Blood Sport, Odds Against, Flying Finish, Slayride, In the Frame,* and *Smokescreen*—all published by Pocket Books.

Books by Dick Francis

Blood Sport
Bonecrack
Dead Cert
Enquiry
Flying Finish
For Kicks
Forfeit
High Stakes
In the Frame
Knockdown
Nerve
Odds Against
Slayride
Smokescreen

Published by POCKET BOOKS

Dick Francis

Bonecrack

PUBLISHED BY POCKET BOOKS NEW YORK

**POCKET BOOKS, a Simon & Schuster division of
GULF & WESTERN CORPORATION**
1230 Avenue of the Americas, New York, N.Y. 10020

Copyright © 1971 by Dick Francis

Published by arrangement with Harper & Row, Publishers

ISBN: 0-671-82159-8

First Pocket Books printing November, 1978

Trademarks registered in the United States and other countries.

Printed in the U.S.A.

Bonecrack

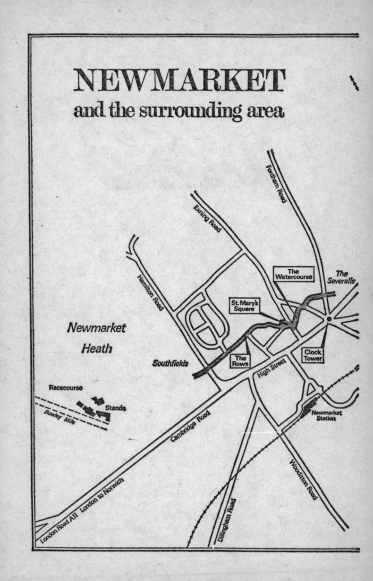

NEWMARKET
and the surrounding area

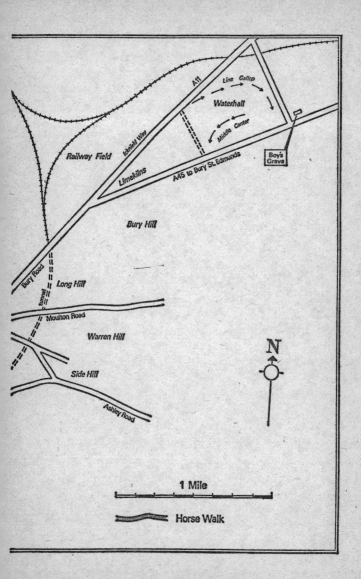

N

1 Mile

〰〰〰〰 Horse Walk

chapter 1

THEY BOTH wore thin rubber masks.

Identical.

I looked at the two identical faceless faces in tingling disbelief. I was not the sort of person to whom rubber-masked individuals, up to no good, paid calls at twenty to midnight. I was a thirty-four-year-old sober-minded businessman quietly bringing up to date the account books at my father's training stables in Newmarket.

The pool of light from the desk lamp shone squarely upon me and the work I had been doing, and the two rubber faces moved palely against the near-black paneling of the dark room like alien moons closing in on the sun. I had looked up when the latch clicked, and there they were, two dim figures calmly walking in from the hall of the big house, silhouetted briefly against the soft lighting behind them and then lost against the paneling as they closed the door. They moved without a squeak, without a scrape, on the bare polished floor. Apart from the unhuman faces, they were black from head to foot.

I picked up the telephone receiver and dialed the first of three nines.

One of the men closed in fast, swung his arm, and smashed downward on the telephone. I removed my finger fractionally in time, with the second nine all but complete, but no one was ever going to achieve the third. The black-gloved hand slowly disentangled a heavy police truncheon from the mangled remains of the post office's property.

"There's nothing to steal," I remarked.

The second man had reached the desk. He stood on the far side of it, looking down at me. He produced an automatic pistol, without silencer, which he pointed unwaveringly at the bridge of my nose. I could see quite a long way into the barrel.

"You," he said. "You will come with us."

His voice was flat, without tone, deliberate. There was no identifiable accent, but he wasn't English.

"Why?"

"You will come."

"Where to?"

"You will come."

"I won't, you know," I said pleasantly, and reached out and pressed the button which switched off the desk lamp.

The sudden total darkness got me two seconds' advantage. I used them to stand up, pick up the heavy angled lamp, and swing the base of it round in an arc in the general direction of the mask which had spoken.

There was a dull thump as the lamp connected, and a grunt. Damage, I thought, but no knockout.

Mindful of the truncheon on my left, I was out from behind the desk and sprinting toward the door. But no one was wasting time batting away in the darkness in the hope of hitting me. A beam of torchlight snapped out from his hand, swung round and dazzled on my face, and bounced as he came after me.

I swerved. Dodged. Lost my straight line to the door and saw sidewise that the rubber face I'd hit with the lamp was purposefully on the move.

The torch beam flickered away, circled briefly, and steadied like a rock on the light switch beside the door. Before I could reach it, the black-gloved hand swept downward and clicked on the five double wall brackets, ten naked candle bulbs coldly lighting the square wood-lined room.

There were two windows with green floor-length curtains. One rug from Istanbul. Three unmatched William and Mary chairs. One sixteenth-century oak chest. One flat walnut desk. Nothing else. An austere place, reflection of my father's austere and Spartan soul.

I had always agreed that the best time to foil an abduction was at the moment it started; that merely obeying marching orders could save present pain but not long-term anxiety; that abductors might kill later but not at the beginning; and that if no one else's safety was at risk, it would be stupid to go without a fight.

Well, I fought.

I fought for all of ninety seconds more, during which time I failed to switch off the lights, to escape through the door, or to crash out through the windows. I had only my hands and not much skill against the truncheon of one of them and the threat of a crippling bullet from the other. The identical rubber faces came toward me with an unnerving lack of human expression, and although I tried, probably unwisely, to rip one of the masks off, I got no further than feeling my fingers slip across the tough slippery surface.

The men favored infighting, with their quarry pinned against the wall. As there were two of them, and they appeared to be experts in their craft, I got such a hammering in that eternal ninety seconds that I soundly wished I had not put my abduction-avoiding theories into practice.

It ended with a fist in my stomach, the pistol slamming into my face, my head crashing back against the paneling, and the truncheon polishing the whole thing off somewhere behind my right ear. When I was next conscious of anything, time had all too clearly passed. Otherwise I should not have been lying face down along the back seat of a moving car with my hands tied crampingly behind my back.

For a good long time, I believed I was dreaming. Then my brain came further awake and made it clear that I wasn't. I was revoltingly uncomfortable and also extremely cold, as the thin sweater I had been wearing indoors was proving a poor barrier to a freezing night.

My head ached with a throb like a steam hammer. Bang, bang, bang. If I could have raised the mental energy, I would have been furious with myself for having proved such a pushover. As it was, only uncomplicated responses were getting anywhere, like dumb unintelligent endurance and a fog-like bewilderment. Of all the candidates for abduction, I would have put myself among the most unlikely.

There was a lot to be said for a semiconscious brain in a semiconscious body. *Mens blotto in corpore ditto....* The words dribbled inconsequentially through my mind, and a smile started along the right nerve but didn't get as far as my mouth. My mouth anyway was half in contact with some imitation leather upholstery which smelled of dogs. They say many grown men call out for their mothers in moments of fatal agony, and then upon their God: but I hadn't had a mother since I was two, and from then until seven I had believed God was someone who had run off with her and was living with her somewhere else. ("God took your mother, dear, because he needed her more than you do"), which had never endeared him to me; and in any case this was no fatal agony, this was just a thumping concussion and some very sore places and maybe a grisly future at the end of the ride. The ride meanwhile went on and on. Nothing about it improved. After several years, the car stopped with a jerk. I nearly fell forward off the seat. My brain came alert with a jolt and my body wished it hadn't.

The two rubber faces loomed over me, lugged me out, and literally carried me up some steps and into a house. One of them had his hands under my armpits and the other held my ankles. My hundred and sixty pounds seemed to be no special burden.

The sudden light inside the door was dazzling, which seemed as good a reason as any for shutting one's eyes. I shut them. The steam hammer had not by any means given up.

They dumped me presently down on my side, on a wooden floor. Polished. I could smell the polish. Scented. Very nasty. I opened my eyes a slit, and verified. Small intricately squared parquet, modern. Birch veneer, wafer thin. Nothing great.

A voice awakening toward fury and controlled with audible effort spoke from a short distance above me.

"And who exactly is this?"

There was a long pin-dropping silence during which I would have laughed if I could. The rubber faces hadn't even pinched the right man. All that battering for bloody nothing. And no guarantee they would take me home again, either.

I squinted upward against the light. The man who had spoken was sitting in an upright leather armchair with his fingers laced rigidly together over a swelling paunch. His voice was much the same as rubber mask's: without much accent, but not English. His shoes, which were more on my level, were supple, handmade, and of Genoese leather.

Italian shape. Not conclusive: they sell Italian shoes from Hong Kong to San Francisco.

One of the rubber faces cleared his throat. "It is Griffon."

The remains of laughter died coldly away. Griffon was indeed my name. If I was not the right man, they must have come for my father. Yet that made no more sense; he was, like me, in none of the abduction-prone professions.

The man in the armchair, with the same reined-in anger, said through his teeth, "It is not Griffon."

"It is," persisted rubber face faintly.

The man stood up out of his armchair and with his elegant toe rolled me over onto my back.

"Griffon is an old man," he said. The sting in his voice sent both rubber faces back a pace as if he had physically hit them.

"You didn't *tell* us he was old," the first one protested. "You didn't describe him. You just told us to bring the trainer from Rowley Lodge."

The other rubber face backed up his colleague in a defensive whine and a different accent. This time, down-the-scale American. "We watched him all evening. He went around the stables, looking at the horses. At every horse. The men, they treated him as boss. He is the trainer. He is Griffon."

"Griffon's assistant," he said furiously. He sat down again and held on to the arms with the same effort as he was holding on to his temper.

"Get up," he said to me abruptly.

I struggled up nearly as far as my knees, but the rest was daunting, and I thought, Why on earth should I bother, so I lay gently down again. It did nothing to improve the general climate.

"Get up," he said furiously.

I shut my eyes.

There was a sharp blow on my thigh. I opened my eyes again in time to see the American-voiced rubber face draw back his foot for another kick. All one could say was that he was wearing shoes and not boots.

"Stop it." The sharp voice arrested him in mid-kick. "Just put him in that chair."

American rubber face picked up the chair in question and placed it six feet from the armchair, facing it. Mid-Victorian, I assessed automatically. Mahogany. Probably once had a caned seat, but was upholstered now in pink

flowered glazed chintz. The two rubber faces lifted me up
bodily and draped me around so that my tied wrists were
behind the back of the chair. When they had done that,
they stepped away, just as far as one pace behind each of
my shoulders.

From that elevation, I had a better view of their master,
if not of the total situation.

"Griffon's assistant," he repeated. But this time, the anger was secondary; he'd accepted the mistake and was
working out what to do about it.

It didn't take him long.

"Gun," he said, and rubber face gave it to him.

He was plump and bald, and I guessed he would take
no pleasure from looking at old photographs of himself.
Under the rounded cheeks, the heavy chin, the folds of
eyelids, there lay an elegant bone structure. It still showed
in the strong clear beak of the nose and in the arch above
the eye sockets. He had the basic equipment of a hand-
some man, but he looked, I thought fancifully, like a Caesar gone self-indulgently to seed, and one might have
taken the fat as a sign of mellowness had it not been for
the ill will that looked unmistakably out of his narrowed
eyes.

"Silencer," he said acidly. He was contemptuous, irritated, and not suffering his rubber-faced fools gladly.

One rubber face produced a silencer from his trouser
pocket and Caesar began screwing it on. Silencers meant
business where naked barrels might not. He was about to
bury his employees' mistake.

My future looked decidedly dim. Time for a few well-
chosen words, especially if they might prove to be my last.

"I am not Griffon's assistant," I said. "I am his son."

He had finished screwing on the silencer and was beginning to raise it in the direction of my chest.

"I am Griffon's son," I repeated. "And just what is the
point of all this?"

The silencer reached the latitude of my heart.

"If you're going to kill me," I said, "you might at least
tell me why."

My voice sounded more or less all right. He couldn't
see, I hoped, that all my skin was prickling into sweat.

I stared at him; he stared back. I waited. Waited while

the tumblers clicked over in his brain, waited for three thumbs down to slot into a row on the fruit machine.

Finally, without lowering the gun a millimeter, he said, "Where is your father?"

"In hospital."

Another pause.

"How long will he be there?"

"I don't know. Two or three months, perhaps."

"Is he dying?"

"No."

"What is the matter with him?"

"He was in a car crash. A week ago. He has a broken leg."

Another pause. The gun was still steady. No one, I thought wildly, should die so unfairly. Yet people did die unfairly. Probably only one in a million deserved it. All death was intrinsically unfair; but in some forms more unfair than in others. Murder, it forcibly seemed to me, was the most unfair of all.

In the end, all he said, and in a much milder tone, was "Who will train the horses this summer if your father is not well enough?"

Only long experience of wily negotiators who thundered big threats so that they could achieve their real aims by presenting them as a toothless anticlimax kept me from stepping straight off the precipice. I nearly, in relief at so harmless an inquiry, told him the truth: that no one had yet decided. If I had done, I discovered later, he would have shot me, because his business was exclusively with the resident trainer at Rowley Lodge. Temporary substitutes, abducted in error, were too dangerous to leave chattering around.

So from instinct I answered, "I will be training them myself," although I had not the slightest intention of doing so for longer than it took to find someone else.

It had indeed been the crucial question. The frightening black circle of the silencer's barrel dipped a fraction; became an ellipse; disappeared altogether. He lowered the gun and balanced it on one well-padded thigh.

A deep breath trickled in and out of my chest in jerks, and the relief from immediate tension made me feel sick. Not that total safety loomed very loftily on the horizon. I was still tied up in an unknown house, and I still had no idea for what possible purpose I could be a hostage.

The fat man went on watching me. Went on thinking. I tried to ease the stiffness which was creeping into my muscles, to shift away the small pains and the throbbing headache, which I hadn't felt in the slightest when faced with a bigger threat.

The room was cold. The rubber faces seemed to be snug enough in their masks and gloves, and the fat man was insulated and impervious, but the chill was definitely adding to my woes. I wondered whether he had planned the cold as a psychological intimidation for my elderly father, or whether it was simply accidental. Nothing in the room looked cozily lived in.

In essence, it was a middle-class sitting room in a small-ish middle-class house, built, I guess, in the nineteen-thirties. The furniture had been pushed back against striped cream wallpaper to give the fat man clear space for maneuver: furniture which consisted of an uninspiring three-piece suite swathed in pink chintz, a gate-leg table, a standard lamp with parchment-colored shade, and a display cabinet displaying absolutely nothing. There were no rugs on the highly polished birch parquet, no ornaments, no books or magazines, nothing personal at all. As bare as my father's soul, but not to his taste.

The room did not in the least fit what I had so far seen of the fat man's personality.

"I will release you," he said, "on certain conditions."

I waited. He considered me, still taking his time.

"If you do not follow my instructions exactly, I will put your father's training stables out of business."

I could feel my mouth opening in astonishment. I shut it with a snap.

"I suppose you doubt that I can do it. Do not doubt. I have destroyed better things than your father's little racing stables."

He got no reaction from me to the slight in the word "little." It was years since I had learned that to rise to slights was to be forced into a defensive attitude which only benefited my opponent. In Rowley Lodge, as no doubt he knew, stood eighty-five aristocrats whose aggregate worth topped six million pounds.

"How?" I asked flatly.

He shrugged. "What is important to you is not how I would do it, but how to prevent me from doing it. And that, of course, is comparatively simple."

"Just run the horses to your instructions?" I suggested neutrally. "Just lose to order?"

A spasm of renewed anger twisted the chubby features and the gun came six inches off his knee. The hand holding it relaxed slowly, and he put it down again.

"I am not," he said heavily, "a petty crook."

But you do, I thought, rise to an insult, even to one that was not intended, and one day, if the game went on long enough, that could give me an advantage.

"I apologize," I said without sarcasm. "But those rubber masks are not top level."

He glanced up in irritation at the two figures standing behind me. "The masks are their own choice. They feel safer if they cannot be recognized."

Like highwaymen, I thought; who swung in the end.

"You may run your horses as you like. You are free to choose entirely . . . save in one special thing."

I made no comment. He shrugged, and went on.

"You will employ someone who I will send you."

"No," I said.

"Yes." He stared at me unwinkingly. "You will employ this person. If you do not, I will destroy the stable."

"That's lunacy," I insisted. "It's pointless."

"No, it is not," he said. "Furthermore, you will tell no one that you are being forced to employ this person. You will assert that it is your own wish. You will particularly not complain to the police, either about tonight or about anything else which may happen. Should you act in any way to discredit this person, or to get him evicted from your stables, your whole business will be destroyed." He paused. "Do you understand? If you act in any way against this person, your father will have nothing to return to when he leaves the hospital."

After a short intense silence, I asked, "In what capacity do you want this person to work for me?"

He answered with care. "He will ride the horses," he said. "He is a jockey."

I could feel the twitch round my eyes. He saw it, too. The first time he had really reached me.

It was out of the question. He would not need to tell me every time he wanted a race lost. He had simply to tell his man.

"We don't need a jockey," I said. "We already have Tommy Hoylake."

"Your new jockey will gradually take his place."

Tommy Hoylake was the second-best jockey in Britain and among the top dozen in the world. No one could take his place.

"The owners wouldn't agree," I said.

"You will persuade them."

"Impossible."

"The future existence of your stable depends on it."

There was another longish pause. One of the rubber faces shifted on his feet and sighed as if from boredom, but the fat man seemed to be in no hurry. Perhaps he understood very well that I was getting colder and more uncomfortable minute by minute. I would have asked him to untie my hands if I hadn't been sure he would count himself one up when he refused.

Finally, I said, "Equipped with your jockey, the stable would have no future existence anyway."

He shrugged. "It may suffer a little, perhaps, but it will survive."

"It is unacceptable," I said.

He blinked. His hand moved the gun gently to and fro across his well-filled trouser leg.

He said, "I see that you do not entirely understand the position. I told you that you could leave here upon certain conditions." His flat tone made the preposterous sound reasonable. "These conditions are that you employ a certain jockey, and that you do not seek aid from anyone, including the police. Should you break either of these agreements, the stable will be destroyed. But"—he spoke more slowly, and with emphasis—"if you do not agree to these conditions in the first place, you will not be freed."

I said nothing.

"Do you understand?"

I sighed. "Yes."

"Good."

"Not a petty crook, I think you said."

His nostrils flared. "I am a manipulator."

"And a murderer."

"I never murder unless the victim insists."

I stared at him. He was laughing inside at his own jolly joke, the fun creeping out in little twitches to his lips and tiny snorts of breath.

This victim, I supposed, was not going to insist. He was welcome to his amusement.

I could believe, all at once, that he was no ordinary crook. Crooked, yes; but something else besides. Something undefinable, unrecognizable, alien. Something . . . *crazy*.

I moved my shoulders slightly, trying to ease them. He watched attentively and offered nothing.

"Who, then, is this jockey?" I said.

He hesitated.

"He is eighteen," he said.

"Eighteen . . ."

He nodded. "You will give him the good horses to ride. He will ride Archangel in the Derby."

Impossible. Totally impossible. I looked at the gun lying so quiet on the expensive tailoring. I said nothing. There was nothing to say.

When he next spoke, there was the satisfaction of victory in his voice alongside the careful non-accent.

"He will arrive at the stable tomorrow. You will hire him. He has not yet much experience in races. You will see he gets it."

An inexperienced rider on Archangel . . . ludicrous. So ludicrous, in fact, that he had used abduction and the threat of murder to make it clear he meant it seriously.

"His name is Alessandro Rivera," he said.

After another interval for consideration, he added the rest of it.

"He is my son."

chapter 2

WHEN I next woke up, I was lying face down on the bare floor of the oak-paneled room in Rowley Lodge. Too many bare boards everywhere. Not my night.

Facts oozed back gradually. I felt woolly, cold, semiconscious, anesthetized....

Anesthetized.

For the return journey, they had had the courtesy not to hit my head. The fat man had nodded to the American rubber face, but instead of flourishing the truncheon he had given me a sort of quick pricking thump in the upper arm. After that, we had waited around for about a quarter of an hour during which no one said anything at all, and then quite suddenly I had lost consciousness. I remembered not a flicker of the journey home.

Creaking and groaning, I tested all articulated parts. Everything present, correct, and in working order. More or less, that is, because having clanked to my feet, it became advisable to sit down again in the chair by the desk. I put my elbows on the desk and my head in my hands, and let time pass.

Outside, the beginnings of a damp dawn were turning the sky to gray flannel. There was ice round the edges of the windows, where condensed warm air had frozen solid. The cold went through to my bones.

In the brain department, things were just as chilly. I remembered all too clearly that Alessandro Rivera was that day to make his presence felt. Perhaps he would take after his father, I thought tiredly, and would be so overweight that the whole dilemma would fold its horns and quietly steal away. On the other hand, if not, why should his father use a sledgehammer to crack a peanut? Why not simply apprentice his son in the normal way? Because he wasn't normal, because his son wouldn't be a normal apprentice, and because no normal apprentice would expect to start his career on a Derby favorite.

I wondered how my father would now be reacting had he not been slung up in traction with a complicated fracture of tibia and fibula. He would not, for certain, be feeling as battered as I was, because he would, with supreme dignity, have gone quietly. But he would nonetheless have also been facing the same vital questions: which were, firstly, did the fat man seriously intend to destroy the stable if his son did not get the job, and secondly, how could he do it?

And the answer to both was a king-sized blank.

It wasn't my stable to risk. They were not my six million pounds' worth of horses. They were not my livelihood, or my life's work.

I could not ask my father to decide for himself; he was not well enough to be told, let alone to reason out the pros and cons.

I could not now transfer the stable to anyone else, because passing this situation to a stranger would be like handing him a grenade with the pin out.

I was already due back at my own job and was late for my next assignment, and I had only stopgapped at the stable at all because my father's capable assistant, who had been driving the Rolls when the lorry jackknifed into it, was now lying in the same hospital in a coma.

All of which added up to a fair-sized problem. But then problems, I reflected ironically, were my business. The problems of sick businesses were my business.

Nothing at that moment looked sicker than my prospects at Rowley Lodge.

Shivering violently, I removed myself bit by bit from the desk and chair, went out to the kitchen, and made myself some coffee. Drank it. Moderate improvement only.

Inched upstairs to the bathroom. Scraped off the night's whiskers and dispassionately observed the dried blood down one cheek. Washed it off. Gun-barrel graze, dry and already healing.

Outside, through the leafless trees, I could see the lights of the traffic thundering as usual up and down Bury Road. Those drivers in their warm moving boxes, they were in another world altogether, a world where abduction and extortion were something that only happened to others. Incredible to think that I had in fact joined the others.

Wincing from an all-over feeling of soreness, I looked

at my smudge-eyed reflection and decided that for a little while at least I would do what the fat man dictated. Partly out of curiosity, partly out of serious concern for the stable, I would wait to see what happened before mounting what might prove to be a self-destructive counterattack. A quieter way out, a profitable solution, would probably reveal itself in the end. It usually did. Meanwhile I would emulate the saplings which bent before the storm ... and lived to grow into oaks.

Long live oaks.

I swallowed some aspirins, stopped shivering, tried to marshal a bit more sense into my shaky wits, and struggled into jodhpurs, boots, two more pullovers, and a windproof jacket. Whatever had happened that night, or whatever might happen in the future, there were still those eighty-five six million quids' worth downstairs waiting to be seen to.

They were housed in a yard that had been an inspiration of spacious design when it was built in 1870 and which still, a hundred-plus years later, worked as an effective unit. Originally there had been two blocks facing each other, each block consisting of three bays, and each bay being made up of ten boxes. Across the far end, forming a wall joining the two blocks, were a large feed storeroom, a pair of double gates, and an equally large tack room. The gates had originally led into a field, but early on in his career, when success struck him, my father had built on two more bays, which formed another small enclosed yard of twenty-five boxes. More double gates opened from these now into a small railed paddock.

Four final boxes had been built facing toward Bury Road, onto the outside of the short west wall at the end of the north block. It was in the farthest of these four boxes that a full-blown disaster had just been discovered.

My appearance through the door which led directly from the house to the yard galvanized the group which had been clustered round the outside boxes into returning into the main yard and advancing in ragged but purposeful formation. I could see I was not going to like their news. Waited in irritation to hear it. Crises, on that particular morning, were far from welcome.

"It's Moonrock, sir," said one of the lads anxiously. "Got cast in his box and broke his leg."

"All right," I said abruptly. "Get back to your own horses, then. It's nearly time to pull out."

"Yes, sir," they said, and scattered reluctantly round the yard to their charges, looking back over their shoulders.

"Damn and bloody hell," I said aloud, but I can't say it did much good. Moonrock was my father's hack, a pensioned-off star-class steeplechaser of which he was uncharacteristically fond. The least valuable inmate of the yard in many terms, but the one he would be most upset to lose. The others were insured. No one, though, could insure against painful emotion.

I plodded round to the box. The elderly lad who looked after him was standing at the door with the light from inside falling across the deep worried wrinkles in his tortoise skin and turning them to crevices. He looked round toward me at my step. The crevices shifted and changed like a kaleidoscope.

"Ain't no good, sir. He's broke his hock."

Nodding, I reached the door and went in. The old horse was standing up, tied in his usual place by his head-collar. At first sight, there was nothing wrong with him: he turned his head toward me and pricked up his ears, his liquid black eyes showing nothing but his customary curiosity. Five years in headline limelight had given him the sort of presence which only intelligent, highly successful horses seem to develop—a sort of consciousness of their own greatness. He knew more about life and about racing than any of the golden youngsters in the main yard. He was fifteen years old and had been a friend of my father's for five.

The hind leg on his near side, toward me, was perfect. He bore his weight on it. The off-hind looked slightly tucked up.

He had been sweating; there were great dark patches on his neck and flanks, but he looked calm enough at that moment. Pieces of straw were caught in his coat, which was unusually dusty.

Soothing him with her hand, and talking to him in a common-sense voice, was my father's head stable hand,

Etty Craig. She looked up at me with regret on her pleasant weather-beaten face.

"I've sent for the vet, Mr. Neil."

"Of all damn things," I said.

She nodded. "Poor old fellow. You'd think he'd know
better after all these years."

I made a sympathetic noise, went in and fondled the
moist black muzzle, and took as good a look at his hind
leg as I could without moving him. There was absolutely
no doubt: the hock joint was out of shape.

Horses occasionally rolled around on their backs in the
straw in their boxes. Sometimes they rolled over with too
little room and wedged their legs against the wall, then
thrashed around to get free. Most injuries from getting
cast were grazes and strains, but it was possible for a
horse to twist or lash out with a leg strongly enough to
break it. Incredibly bad luck when it happened, which
luckily wasn't often.

"He was still lying down when George came in to muck
him out," Etty said. "He got some of the lads to come and
pull the old fellow into the center of the box. He was a bit
slow, George says, standing up. And then of course they
could see he couldn't walk."

"Bloody shame," George said, nodding in agreement.

I sighed. "Nothing we can do, Etty."

"No, Mr. Neil."

She called me Mr. Neil religiously during working
hours, though I'd been plain Neil to her in my childhood.
Better for discipline in the yard, she said to me once, and
on matters of discipline I would never contradict her.
There had been quite a stir in Newmarket when my father
had promoted her to head lad, but as he had explained to
her at the time, she was loyal, she was knowledgeable, she
would stand no nonsense from anyone. She deserved it
from seniority alone, and had she been a man the job
would have been hers automatically. He had decided, as
he was a just and logical person, that her sex was immate-
rial. She became the only female head lad in Newmarket—where girl lads, anyway, were rare—and the stable
had flourished through all the six years of her reign.

I remembered the days when her parents used to turn
up at the stables and accuse my father of ruining her life.

I had been about ten when she first came to the yard, and she was nineteen and had been privately educated at an expensive boarding school. Her parents with increasing bitterness had complained that the stable was spoiling her chances of a nice suitable marriage; but Etty had never wanted marriage. If she had ever experimented with sex, she had not made a public mess of it, and I thought it likely that she had found the whole process uninteresting. She seemed to like males well enough, but she treated them as she did her horses, with brisk friendliness, immense understanding, and cool unsentimentality.

Since my father's accident, she had to all intents been in complete charge. The fact that I had been granted a temporary license to hold the fort made mine the official say-so, but both Etty and I knew I would be lost without her.

It occurred to me, as I watched her capable hands moving quietly across Moonrock's bay hide, that the fat man might think me a pushover, but as an apprentice his son Alessandro was going to run into considerable difficulties with Miss Henrietta Craig.

"You better go out with the string, Etty," I said. "I'll stay and wait for the vet."

"Right," she said, and I guessed she had been on the point of suggesting it herself. As a distribution of labor, it was only sense, for the horses were well along in their preparation for the coming racing season, and she knew better than I what each should be doing.

She beckoned to George to come and hold Moonrock's head-collar and keep him soothed. To me she said, stepping out of the box, "What about this frost? It seems to me it may be thawing."

"Take the horses over to Warren Hill and use your own judgment about whether to canter."

She nodded. "Right." She looked back at Moonrock, and a momentary softness touched her mouth. "Mr. Griffon will be sorry."

"I won't tell him yet."

"No." She gave me a small businesslike smile and walked off into the yard, a short neat figure, hardy and competent.

Moonrock would be quiet enough with George. I followed Etty back into the main yard and watched the horses pull out: thirty-three of them in the first lot. The lads led their charges out of the boxes, jumped up into the saddles, and rode away down the yard, through the first double gates, across the lower yard, and out through the far gates into the collecting paddock beyond. The sky lightened moment by moment, and I thought Etty was probably right about the thaw.

After ten minutes or so, when she had sorted them out as she wanted them, the horses moved away out beyond the paddock, through the trees and the boundary fence, and straight out onto the Heath.

Before the last of them had gone, there was a rushing scrunch in the drive behind me and the vet halted his dusty Land-Rover with a spray of gravel. Leaping out with his bag, he said breathlessly, "Every bloody horse on the Heath this morning has got colic or ingrowing toenails. You must be Neil Griffon. Sorry about your father. Etty says it's old Moonrock. Still in the same box?" Without drawing breath, he turned on his heel and strode along the outside boxes. Young, chubby, purposeful, he was not the vet I had expected. The man I knew was an older version, slower, twinkly, just as chubby, and given to rubbing his jaw while he thought things over.

"Sorry about this," Dainsee, the young vet, said, having given Moonrock three full seconds of examination. "Have to put him down, I'm afraid."

"I suppose that hock couldn't just be dislocated?" I suggested, clinging to straws.

He gave me a brief glance full of the expert's forgiveness for a layman's ignorance. "The joint is shattered," he said succinctly.

He went about his business, and splendid old Moonrock quietly folded down onto the straw. Packing his bag again, the vet said, "Don't look so depressed. He had a better life than most. And be glad it wasn't Archangel."

I watched his chubby back depart at speed. Not so very unlike his father, I thought. Just faster.

I went slowly into the house and telephoned to the people who removed dead horses. They would come at once, they said, sounding cheerful. And within half an hour, they came.

Another cup of coffee. Sat down beside the kitchen table and went on feeling unwell. Abduction didn't agree with me in the least.

The string came back from the Heath without Etty, without a two-year-old colt called Lucky Lindsay, and with a long tale of woe.

I listened with increasing dismay while three lads at once told me that Lucky Lindsay had whipped round and unshipped little Ginge over by Warren Hill, and had then galloped off loose and seemed to be making for home, but had diverted down Moulton Road instead, and had knocked over a man with a bicycle and had sent a woman with a pram into hysterics, and had ended up by the clock tower, disorganizing the traffic. The police, added one boy, with more relish than regret, were currently talking to Miss Etty.

"And the colt?" I asked. Because Etty could take care of herself, but Lucky Lindsay had cost thirty thousand guineas and could not.

"Someone caught him down the High Street outside Woolworth's."

I sent them off to their horses and waited for Etty to come back, which she presently did, riding Lucky Lindsay herself and with the demoted and demoralized Ginge slopping along behind on a quiet three-year-old mare.

Etty jumped down and ran an experienced hand down the colt's chestnut legs.

"Not much harm done," she said. "He seems to have a small cut there. . . . I think he probably did it on the bumper of a parked car."

"Not on the bicycle?" I asked.

She looked up, and then straightened. "Shouldn't think so."

"Was the cyclist hurt?"

"Shaken," she admitted.

"And the woman with the pram?"

"Anyone who pushes a baby and drags a toddler along Moulton Road during morning exercise should be ready for loose horses. The stupid woman wouldn't stop screaming. It upset the colt thoroughly, of course. Someone had caught him at that point, but he backed off and broke free and went down into the town."

She paused and looked at me. "Sorry about all this."

"It happens," I said. I stifled the small inward smile at her relative placing of colts and babies. Not surprising. To her, colts were, in sober fact, more important than humans.

"We had finished the canters," she said. "The ground was all right. We went right through the list we mapped out yesterday. Ginge came off as we turned for home."

"Is the colt too much for him?"

"Wouldn't have thought so. He's ridden him before."

"I'll leave it to you, Etty."

"Then maybe I'll switch him to something easier for a day or two." She led the colt away and handed him over to the lad who did him, having come as near as she was likely to admitting she had made an error in putting Ginge on Lucky Lindsay. Anyone, any day, could be thrown off. But some were thrown off more than others.

Breakfast. The lads put straight the horses they had just ridden, and scurried round to the hostel for porridge, bacon sandwiches, and tea. I went back into the house and didn't feel like eating.

It was still cold indoors. There were sad mounds of fir cones in the fireplaces of ten dust-sheeted bedrooms, and a tapestry fire screen in front of the hearth in the drawing room. There was a two-tier electric fire in the cavernous bedroom my father used and an undersized convector heater in the oak-paneled room where he sat at his desk in the evenings. Not even the kitchen was warm, as the cooker fire had been out for repairs for a month. Normally, having been brought up in it, I did not notice the chill of the house in winter; but then normally I did not feel so physically wretched.

A head appeared round the kitchen door. Neat dark hair coiled smoothly at the base, to emerge in a triumphant arrangement of piled curls on the crown.

"Mr. Neil?"

"Oh . . . good morning, Margaret."

A pair of fine dark eyes gave me an embracing once-over. Narrow nostrils moved in a small quiver, testing the atmosphere. As usual, I could see no further than her neck and half a cheek; my father's secretary was as economical with her presence as with everything else.

"It's cold in here," she said.

"Yes."

"Warmer in the office."

The half head disappeared and did not come back. I decided to accept what I knew had been meant as an invitation, and retraced my way toward the corner of the house which adjoined the yard. In that corner were the stable office, a cloakroom, and the one room furnished for comfort, the room we called the owners' room, where owners and assorted others were entertained on casual visits to the stable.

The lights were on in the office, bright against the gray day outside. Margaret was taking off her sheepskin coat, and hot air was blowing busily out of a mushroom-shaped heater.

"Instructions?" she asked briefly.

"I haven't opened the letters yet."

She gave me a quick comprehensive glance.

"Trouble?"

I told her about Moonrock and Lucky Lindsay. She listened attentively, showed no emotion, and asked how I had cut my face.

"Walked into a door."

Her expression said plainly, "I've heard that one before," but she made no comment.

In her way, she was as unfeminine as Etty, despite her skirt, her hairdo, and her efficient make-up. In her late thirties, three years widowed, and bringing up a boy and a girl with masterly organization, she bristled with intelligence and held the world at arm's length from her heart.

Margaret was new at Rowley Lodge, replacing mouse-like old Robinson, who had finally scratched his way at seventy into unwilling retirement. Old Robinson had liked his little chat, and had frittered away hours of working time telling me in my childhood about the days when Charles II rode in races himself, and made Newmarket the second capital of England, so that ambassadors had to go there to see him, and how the Prince Regent had left the town forever because of an inquiry into the running of his colt Escape, and refused to go back even though the

Jockey Club apologized and begged him to, and how in
1905 King Edward VII was in trouble with the police for
speeding down the road to London—at forty miles an
hour on the straight bits.

Margaret did old Robinson's work more accurately and
in half the time, and I understood after knowing her for
six days why my father found her inestimable. She demanded no human response, and he was a man who
found most human relationships boring. Nothing tired him
quicker than people who constantly demanded attention
for their emotions and problems, and even social openers
about the weather irritated him. Margaret seemed to be a
matched soul, and they got on excellently.

I slouched down in my father's revolving office armchair and told Margaret to open the letters herself. My father never let anyone open his letters, and was obsessive
about it. She simply did as I said without comment, either
spoken or implied. Marvelous.

The telephone rang. Margaret answered it.

"Mr. Bredon? Oh, yes. He'll be glad you called. I'll put
you on to him."

She handed me the receiver across the desk, and said,
"John Bredon."

"Thanks."

I took the receiver with none of the eagerness I would
have shown the day before. I had spent three intense days
trying to find someone who was free at short notice to
take over Rowley Lodge until my father's leg mended,
and of all the people helpful friends had suggested, only
John Bredon, an elderly recently retired trainer, seemed to
be of the right experience and caliber. He had asked for
time to think it over and had said he would let me know
as soon as he could.

He was calling to say he would be happy to come. I
thanked him and uncomfortably apologized as I put him
off. "The fact is that after thinking it over I've decided to
stay on myself. . . ."

I set the receiver down slowly, aware of Margaret's astonishment. I didn't explain. She didn't ask. After a
pause, she went back to opening the letters.

The telephone rang again. This time, with schooled features, she asked if I would care to speak to Mr. Russell Arletti.

Silently I stretched out a hand for the receiver.

"Neil?" a voice barked. "Where the hell have you got to? I told Grey & Cox you'd be there yesterday. They're complaining. How soon can you get up there?"

Grey & Cox, in Huddersfield, were waiting for Arletti, Incorporated, to sort out why their once profitable business was going down the drain. Arletti's sorter was sitting disconsolately in a stable office in Newmarket wishing he was dead.

"You'll have to tell Grey & Cox that I can't come."

"You *what?*"

"Russell . . . count me out for a while. I've got to stay on here."

"For God's sake, why?"

"I can't find anyone to take over."

"You said it wouldn't take you more than a week."

"Well, it has. There isn't anyone suitable. I can't go and sort out Grey & Cox and leave Rowley Lodge rudderless. There is six million involved here. Like it or not, I'll have to stay."

"Damn it, Neil . . ."

"I'm really sorry."

"Grey & Cox will be livid." He was exasperated.

"Go up there yourself. It'll only be the usual thing. Bad costing. Underpricing their product at the planning stage. Rotten cash flow. They say they haven't any militants, so it's ninety percent to a cornflake that it's lousy finance."

He sighed. "I don't have quite your talent. Better ones, mind you. But not the same." He paused for thought. "Have to send James, when he gets back from Shoreham. If you're sure?"

"Better count me out for three months at least."

"Neil!"

"Better say, in fact, until after the Derby. . . ."

"Legs don't take that long," he protested.

"This one is a terrible mess. The bones were splintered and came through the skin, and it was touch and go whether they amputated."

"Oh, *hell.*"

"I'll give you a call," I said. "As soon as I look like being free."

After he had rung off, I sat with the receiver in my hand, staring into space. Slowly I put it back in its cradle.

Margaret sat motionless, her eyes studiously downcast, her mouth showing nothing. She made no reference at all to the lie I had told.

It was, I reflected, only the first of many.

chapter 3

NOTHING ABOUT that day got any better.

I rode out with the second lot on the Heath and found there were tender spots I hadn't even known about. Etty asked if I had a toothache. I looked liked it, she said. Sort of drawn, she said.

I said my molars were in good crunching order and how about starting the canters. The canters were started, watched, assessed, repeated, discussed. Archangel, Etty said, would be ready for the Guineas.

When I told her I was going to stay on myself as the temporary trainer, she looked horrified.

"But you *can't*."

"You are unflattering, Etty."

"Well, I mean ... you don't know the horses." She stopped and tried again. "You hardly ever go racing. You've never been really interested, not since you were a boy. You don't know enough about it."

"I'll manage," I said, "with your help."

But she was only slightly reassured, because she was not vain, and she never overestimated her own abilities. She knew she was a good head lad. She knew there was a lot to training that she wouldn't do so well. Such self-knowledge in the sport of kings was rare, and facing it rarer still. There was always thousands of people who knew better, on the stands.

"Who will do the entries?" she asked astringently, her voice saying quite clearly that I couldn't.

"Father can do them himself when he's a bit better. He'll have a lot of time."

At this she nodded with more satisfaction. The entering of horses in races suited to them was the most important skill in training. All the success and prestige of a stable started with the entry forms, where for each individual horse the aim had to be not too high, not too low, but just right. Most of my father's success had been built on his judgment of where to enter and when to run each horse.

One of the two-year-olds pranced around, lashed out, and caught another two-year-old on the knee. The boys' reactions had not been quick enough to keep them apart, and the second colt was walking lame. Etty cursed them coldly and told the second boy to dismount and lead his charge home.

I watched him following on foot behind the string, the horse's head ducking at every tender step. The knee would swell and fill and get hot, but with a bit of luck it would right itself in a few days. If it did not, someone would have to tell the owner. The someone would be me.

That made one horse dead and two damaged in one morning. If things went on at that rate, there would soon be no stable left for the fat man to bother about.

When we got back, there was a small police car in the drive and a large policeman in the office. He was sitting in my chair and staring at his boots, and rose purposefully to his feet as I came through the door.

"Mr. Griffon?"

"Yes."

He came to the point without preliminaries.

"We've had a complaint, sir, that one of your horses knocked over a cyclist on the Moulton Road this morning. Also a young woman has complained to us that this same horse endangered her life and that of her children."

He was a uniformed sergeant, about thirty, solidly built, uncompromising. He spoke with the aggressive politeness that in some policemen is close to rudeness, and I gathered that his sympathies were with the complainants.

"Was the cyclist hurt, Sergeant?"

"I understand he was bruised, sir."

"And his bicycle?"

"I couldn't say, sir."

"Do you think that a—er—a settlement out of court, so to speak, would be in order?"

"I couldn't say, sir," he repeated flatly. His face was full of the negative attitude which erects a barrier against sympathy or understanding. Into my mind floated one of the axioms that Russell Arletti lived by. In business matters with trade unions, the press, or the police, never try to make them like you. It arouses antagonism instead. And never make jokes; they are anti-jokes.

I gave the sergeant back a stare of equal indifference and asked if he had the cyclist's name and address. After only the slightest hesitation, he flicked over a page or two of notebook and read it out to me. Margaret took it down.

"And the young woman's?"

He provided that, too. He then asked if he might take a statement from Miss Craig, and I said certainly, Sergeant, and took him out into the yard. Etty gave him a rapid adding-up inspection and answered his questions in an unemotional manner. I left them together and went back to the office to finish the paperwork with Margaret, who preferred to work straight through the lunch hour and leave at three to collect her children from school.

"Some of the account books are missing," she observed.

"I had them last night," I said. "They're in the oak room. . . . I'll go and fetch them."

The oak room was quiet and empty. I wondered what reaction I would get from the sergeant if I brought him in and said that last night two faceless men had knocked me out, tied me up, and removed me from my home by force. Also they had threatened to kill me, and had punched me full of anesthetic to bring me back.

"Oh, yes, sir? And do you want to make a formal allegation?"

I smiled slightly. It seemed ridiculous. The sergeant would produce a stare of top-grade disbelief, and I could hardly blame him. Only my depressing state of health and the smashed telephone lying on the desk made the night's events seem real at all.

The fat man, I reflected, hardly needed to have warned me away from the police. The sergeant had done the job for him. It would have been sensible, I supposed, to have enlisted help—if not from the sergeant, at least from one of his superiors. I knew it wasn't only the risk to the stable which stopped me, or the sergeant's off-putting manner, but something more obscure and internal, some urge to deal with the situation myself. To calm things down, rather than stir them up. Wait and see, I thought. Wait and see.

Etty came into the office fuming while I was returning the account books to Margaret.

"Of all the pompous clods!"

"Does this sort of thing happen often?" I asked.

"Of course not," Etty said positively. "Horses get loose, of course, but things are usually settled without all this

fuss. And I told that old man that you would see he didn't
suffer. Why he had to go complaining to the police beats
me."

"I'll go and see him this evening," I said.

"Now, the old sergeant, Sergeant Chubb," Etty said
forcefully, "he would have sorted it out himself. He
wouldn't have come round taking down statements. But
this one—this one is new here. They've posted him here
from Ipswich, and he doesn't seem to like it. Just promoted,
I shouldn't wonder. Full of his own importance."

"The stripes were new," Margaret murmured in agreement.

"We always have good relations with the police here,"
Etty said gloomily. "Can't think what they're doing, sending the town someone who doesn't understand the first
thing about horses."

The steam had all blown off. Etty breathed sharply
through her nose, shrugged her shoulders, and produced a
small resigned smile.

"Oh, well . . . worse things happen at sea."

She had very blue eyes, and light brown hair that went
frizzy when the weather was damp. Middle age had
roughened her skin without wrinkling it, and as with most
undersexed women there was much in her face that was
male. She had thin dry lips and bushy unkempt eyebrows,
and the handsomeness of her youth was only something I
remembered. Etty seemed a sad, wasted person to many
who observed her, but to herself she was fulfilled, and was
busily content.

She stamped away in her jodhpurs and boots, and we
heard her voice raised at some luckless boy caught in
wrongdoing.

Rowley Lodge needed Etty Craig. But it needed
Alessandro Rivera like a hole in the head.

He came late that afternoon.

I was out in the yard looking round the horses at evening stables. With Etty alongside, I had got as far as bay
five, from where we would go round the bottom yard before walking up again toward the house.

One of the fifteen-year-old apprentices nervously appeared as we came out of a box and prepared to go into the next.

"Someone to see you, sir."

"Who?"

"Don't know, sir."

"An owner?"

"Don't know, sir."

"Where is he?"

"Up by the drive, sir."

I looked up, over his head. Beyond the yard, out on the gravel, there was parked a large white Mercedes with a uniformed chauffeur standing by the bonnet.

"Take over, Etty, would you?" I said.

I walked up through the yard and out into the drive. The chauffeur folded him arms and his mouth like barricades against fraternization. I stopped a few paces away from him and looked toward the inside of the car.

One of the rear doors, the one nearest to me, opened. A small black-shod foot appeared, and then a dark trouser leg, and then, slowly straightening, the whole man.

It was clear at once who he was, although the resemblance to his father began and ended with the autocratic beak of the nose and the steadfast stoniness of the black eyes. The son was emaciated instead of chubby. He had sallow skin that looked in need of a sun tan, and strong thick black hair curving in springy curls round his ears. Over all he wore an air of disconcerting maturity, and the determination in the set of his mouth would have done credit to a steel trap. Eighteen he might be, but it was a long time since he had been a boy.

I guessed that his voice would be like his father's: definite, unaccented, and careful.

It was.

"I am Rivera," he announced. "Alessandro."

"Good evening," I said, and intended it to sound polite, cool, and unimpressed.

He blinked.

"Rivera," he repeated. "I am Rivera."

"Yes," I agreed. "Good evening."

He looked at me with narrowing attention. If he expected from me a lot of groveling, he was not going to get it. And something of this message must have got across to him from my attitude, because he began to look faintly surprised and a shade more arrogant.

"I understand you wish to become a jockey," I said.

"Intend."

I nodded casually. "No one succeeds as a jockey without determination," I said, and made it sound patronizing.

He detected the flavor immediately. He didn't like it. I was glad.

"I am accustomed to succeed," he said.

"How very nice," I replied dryly.

It sealed between us an absolute antagonism. I felt him shift gear into overdrive, and it seemed to me that he was mentally gathering himself to fight on his own account a battle he believed his father had already won.

"I will start at once," he said.

"I am in the middle of evening stables," I said matter-of-factly. "If you will wait, we will discuss your position when I have finished." I gave him the politeness of an inclination of the head which I would have given to anybody, and without waiting around for him to throw any more of his slight weight about, I turned smoothly away and walked without haste back to Etty.

When we had worked our way methodically round to the whole stable, discussing briefly how each horse was progressing, and planning the work program for the following morning, we came finally to the four outside boxes, only three busy now, and the fourth full of Moonrock's absence.

The Mercedes still stood on the gravel, with both Rivera and the chauffeur sitting inside it. Etty gave them a look of regulation curiosity and asked who they were.

"New customer," I said economically.

She frowned in surprise. "But surely you shouldn't have kept him waiting!"

"This one," I reassured her with private, rueful irony, "will not go away."

But Etty knew how to treat new clients, and making them wait in their car was not it. She hustled me along the last three boxes and anxiously pushed me to return to the Mercedes. Tomorrow, no doubt, she would not be so keen.

I opened the rear door and said to him, "Come along into the office."

He climbed out of the car and followed me without a word. I switched on the fan heater, sat in Margaret's chair behind the desk, and pointed to the swivel armchair in front of it. He did as I suggested.

"Now," I said, in my best interviewing voice, "you want to start tomorrow."

"Yes."

"In what capacity?"

He hesitated. "As a jockey."

"Well, no," I said reasonably. "There are no races yet. The season does not start for about four weeks."

"I know that," he said stiffly.

"What I meant was, do you want to work in the stable? Do you want to look after two horses, as the others do?"

"Certainly not."

"Then what?"

"I will ride the horses at exercise two or three times a day. Every day. I will not clean their boxes or carry their food. I wish only to ride."

Highly popular, that was going to be, with Etty and the other lads. Apart from all else, I was going to have a shop floor-management confrontation—or, in plain old terms, a mutiny—on my hands in no time at all. None of the other lads was going to muck out and groom a horse for the joy of seeing Rivera ride it.

However, all I said was "How much experience, exactly, have you had so far?"

"I can ride," he said flatly.

"Race horses?"

"I can ride."

This was getting nowhere. I tried again. "Have you ever ridden in any sort of race?"

"I have ridden in amateur races."

"Where?"

"In Italy, and in Germany."

"Have you won any?"

He gave me a black stare. "I have won two."

I supposed that that was something. At least it suggested that he could stay on. Winning itself, in his case, had no significance. His father was the sort to buy the favorite and nobble the opposition.

"But you want now to become a professional?"

"Yes."

"Then I'll apply for a license for you."

"I can apply myself."

I shook my head. "You will have to have an apprentice license, and I will have to apply for it for you."

"I do not wish to be an apprentice."

I said patiently, "Unless you become an apprentice, you will be unable to claim a weight allowance. In England in flat races, the only people who can claim weight allowances are apprentices. Without a weight allowance, the owners of the horses will all resist to the utmost any suggestion that you should ride. Without weight allowance, in fact, you might as well give up the whole idea."

"My father—" he began.

"Your father can threaten until he's blue in the face," I interrupted. "I cannot *force* the owners to employ you. I can only persuade. Without a weight allowance, they will never be persuaded."

He thought it over, his expression showing nothing.

"My father," he said, "told me that anyone could apply for a license and that there was no need to be apprenticed."

"Technically, that is true."

"But practically, it is not." It was a statement more than a question; he had clearly understood what I had said.

I began to speculate about the strength of his intentions. It certainly seemed possible that if he read the Deed of Apprenticeship and saw to what he would be binding himself, he might simply step back into his car and be driven away. I fished around in Margaret's tidy desk drawers, and found a pile of copies of the printed agreement.

"You will need to sign this," I said casually, and handed one over.

He read it without a flicker of an eyelid, and, considering what he was reading, that was remarkable.

The familiar words trotted through my mind ". . . the Apprentice will faithfully, diligently and honestly serve the Master and obey and perform all his lawful commands

... and will not absent himself from the service of the Master, nor divulge any of the secrets of the Master's business ... and shall deliver to the Master all such monies and other things that shall come into his hands for work done ... and will in all matters and things whatsoever demean and behave himself as a good true and faithful Apprentice ought to do...."

He put the form down on the desk and looked across at me.

"I cannot sign that."

"Your father will have to sign it as well," I pointed out.

"He will not."

"Then that's an end to it," I said, relaxing back in my chair.

He looked down at the form. "My father's lawyers will draw up a different agreement," he said.

I shrugged. "Without a recognizable apprenticeship deed, you won't get an apprentice's license. That form there is based on the articles of apprenticeship common to all trades since the Middle Ages. If you alter its intentions, it won't meet the licensing requirements."

After a packed pause, he said, "That part about delivering all monies to the Master ... does that mean I would have to give to you all money I might earn in races?" He sounded incredulous, as well he might.

"It does say that," I agreed, "but it is normal nowadays for the Master to return half of race earnings to the apprentice. In addition, of course, to giving him a weekly allowance."

"If I win the Derby on Archangel, you would take half. Half of the fee and half of the present?"

"That's right."

"It's wicked!"

"You've got to win it before you start worrying," I said flippantly, and watched the arrogance flare up like a bonfire.

"If the horse is good enough, I will."

You kid yourself, mate, I thought; and didn't answer.

He stood up abruptly, picked up the form, and without another word walked out of the office, and out of the house, out of the yard, and into his car. The Mercedes purred away with him down the drive, and I stayed sitting back in Margaret's chair, hoping I had seen the last of him, wincing at the energy of my persisting headache, and wondering whether a triple brandy would restore me to instant health.

I tried it.

It didn't.

There was no sign of him in the morning, and on all counts the day was better. The kicked two-year-old's knee had gone up like a football but he was walking pretty sound on it, and the cut on Lucky Lindsay was as superficial as Etty had hoped. The elderly cyclist, the evening before, had accepted my apologies and ten pounds for his bruises and had left me with the impression that we could knock him down again, any time, for a similar supplement to his income. Archangel worked a half-speed six furlongs on the Side Hill gallop, and in me a night's sleep had ironed out some creases.

But Alessandro Rivera did come back.

He rolled up the drive in the chauffeur-driven Mercedes just as Etty and I finished the last three boxes at evening stables, timing it so accurately that I wondered if he had been waiting and watching from out on Bury Road.

I jerked my head toward the office, and he followed me in. I switched on the heater and sat down, as before; and so did he.

He produced from an inner pocket the apprenticeship form and passed it toward me across the desk. I took it and unfolded it, and turned it over.

There were no alterations. It was the deed in the exact form he had taken it. There were, however, four additions.

The signatures of Alessandro Rivera and Enso Rivera, with an appropriate witness in each case, sat squarely in the spaces designed for them.

I looked at the bold heavy strokes of both the Riveras' signatures and the nervous elaborations of the witnesses. They had signed the agreement without filling in any of the blanks: without even discussing the time the apprenticeship was to run for, or the weekly allowance to be paid.

He was watching me. I met his cold black eyes.

"You and your father signed it like this," I said slowly, "because you have not the slightest intention of being bound by it."

His face didn't change. "Think what you like," he said.

And so I would. And what I thought was that the son was not as criminal as his father. The son had taken the legal obligations of the apprenticeship form seriously. But his father had not.

chapter 4

THE SMALL private room in the North London hospital where my father had been taken after the crash seemed to be almost entirely filled with the frames and ropes and pulleys and weights which festooned his high bed. Apart from all that, there was only a high-silled window with limp floral curtains and a view of half the back of another building and a chunk of sky, a chest-high washbasin with lever-type taps designed to be turned on by elbows, a bedside locker upon which reposed his lower teeth in a glass of water, and an armchair of sorts, visitors for the use of.

There were no flowers glowing against the margarine-colored walls, and no well-wishing cards brightening the top of the locker. He did not care for flowers, and would have dispatched any that came straight along to the other wards, and I doubted that anyone at all would have made the error of sending him a glossy or amusing get-well, which he would have considered most frightfully vulgar.

The room itself was meager compared with what he would have chosen and could afford, but to me during the first critical days the hospital itself had seemed effortlessly efficient. It did after all, as one doctor had casually explained to me, have to deal constantly with wrecked bodies prized out of crashes on the A1. They were used to it. Geared to it. They had a higher proportion of accident cases than of the normally sick.

He had said he thought I was wrong to insist on private treatment for my father and that he would find time hanging less heavy in a public ward where there was a lot going on, but I had assured him that he did not know my father. He had shrugged and acquiesced, but said that the private rooms weren't much. And they weren't. They were for getting out of quickly, if one could.

When I visited my father that evening, he was asleep. The ravages of the pain he had endured during the past week had deepened and darkened the lines round his eyes and tinged all his skin with gray, and he looked defenseless in a way he never did when he was awake. With his teeth out, the dogmatic set of his mouth was relaxed, and with his eyes shut he no longer seemed to be disapproving of nineteen-twentieths of what occurred. A lock of gray-white hair curved softly down over his forehead, giving him a friendly gentle look which was hopelessly misleading.

He had not been a kind father. I had spent most of my childhood fearing him, and most of my teens loathing him, and only in the past very few years had I come to understand him. The severity with which he had used me had not, after all, been rejection and dislike, but lack of imagination and an inability to love. He had not believed in beating, but he had lavishly handed out other punishments of deprivation and solitude, without realizing that what would have been trifling to him was torment to me. Being locked in one's bedroom for three or four days at a time might not have come under the heading of active cruelty, but it had dumped me into agonies of humiliation and shame; and it had not been possible, although I had tried until I was the most repressed child in Newmarket, to avoid committing anything my father could interpret as a fault.

He had sent me to Eton, which in its way had proved just as callous, and on my sixteenth birthday I ran away.

I knew that he had never forgiven me. An aunt had relayed to me his furious comment that he had provided me with horses to ride and taught me obedience, and what more could any father do for his son?

He had made no effort to get me back, and through all the years of my commercial success we had not once spoken to each other. During that time, I had of course read about him often in the newspapers, and in fact had seen him from a distance several times, as I had never lost my inborn interest in racing, and had occasionally been to race meetings where he had runners. In the end, after fourteen years of avoiding him, I had gone to Ascot knowing that he would be there and wanting finally to make peace.

When I said, "Mr. Griffon . . . ," he had turned to me from a group of people, raised his eyebrows, and looked at me inquiringly. His eyes were cool and blank. He hadn't known me.

I had said, with more amusement than awkwardness, "I am your son. . . . I am Neil."

Apart from surprise, he had shown no emotion whatsoever, and on the tacit understanding that none would be expected on either side, he had suggested that any day I happened to be passing through Newmarket, I could call in and see him.

I had called three or four times every year since then, sometimes for a drink, sometimes for lunch, but never staying; and I had come to see him from a much saner perspective in my thirties than I had at fifteen. His manner to me was still for the most part forbidding, critical, and punitive, but as I no longer depended solely upon him for approval, and as he could no longer lock me in my bedroom for disagreeing with him, I found a perverse sort of pleasure in his company.

I had thought when I was called in a hurry to Rowley Lodge after the accident that I wouldn't sleep again in my old bed, that I'd choose any other. But in fact in the end I did sleep in it, because it was the room that had been prepared for me, and there were dust sheets still over all the rest.

Too much had crowded back when I looked at the unchanged furnishings and the fifty-times-read books on the small bookshelf; and, smile at myself as cynically as I would, on that first night back I hadn't been able to lie in there in the dark with the door shut.

I sat down in the armchair and read the copy of the *Times* which rested on his bed. His hand, yellowish, freckled, and with thick knotted veins, lay limply on the sheets, still half entwined in the black-framed spectacles he had removed before sleeping. I remembered that when I was seventeen I had taken to wearing frames like those, with plain glass in them, because to me they stood for authority, and I had wanted to present an older and weightier personality to my clients. Whether it was the frames or not which did the trick, the antiques business had flourished.

He stirred, and groaned, and the lax hand closed convulsively into a fist with almost enough force to break the lenses.

I stood up. His face was screwed up with pain, and beads of sweat stood out on his forehead, but he sensed that there was someone in the room and opened his eyes sharp and wide as if there were nothing the matter.

"Oh . . . it's you."

"I'll fetch a nurse," I said.

"No. Be better . . . in a minute."

But I went to fetch one anyway, and she looked at the watch pinned upside down on her bosom and remarked that it was time for his pills, near enough.

After he had swallowed them and the worst of it had passed, I noticed that during the short time I was out of the room he had managed to replace his lower teeth. The glass of water stood empty on the locker. A great one for his dignity, my father.

"Have you found anyone to take over the license?" he asked.

"Can I make your pillows more comfortable?" I suggested.

"Leave them alone," he snapped. "Have you found anyone to take charge?" He would go on asking, I knew, until I gave him a direct answer.

"No," I said. "There's no need."

"What do you mean?"

"I've decided to stay on myself."

His mouth opened, just as Etty's had done, and then shut again with equal vigor.

"You can't. You don't know a damn thing about it. You couldn't win a single race."

"The horses are good, Etty is good, and you can sit here and do the entries."

"You will not take over. You will get someone who is capable, someone I approve of. The horses are far too valuable to have amateurs messing about. You will do as I say. Do you hear? You will do as I say."

The pain-killing drug had begun to act on his eyes, if not yet on his tongue.

"The horses will come to no harm," I said, and thought of Moonrock and Lucky Lindsay and the kicked two-year-old, and wished with all my heart I could hand the whole lot over to Bredon that very day.

"If you think," he said with a certain malice, "that be-

cause you can sell antiques you can run a racing stable,
you are overestimating yourself."

"I no longer sell antiques," I pointed out calmly. As he
knew perfectly well.

"The principles are different," he said.

"The principles of all businesses are the same."

"Rubbish."

"Get the costs right and supply what the customer
wants."

"I can't see you supplying winners." He was contemptuous.

"Well," I said moderately, "I can't see why not."

"Can't you?" he asked acidly. "Can't you, indeed?"

"Not if you will give me your advice."

He gave me instead a long wordless stare while he
searched for an adequate answer. The pupils in his gray
eyes had contracted to micro-dots. There was no tension
left in the muscles which had stiffened his jaw.

"You must get someone else," he said; but the words
had begun to slur. I made a noncommittal movement of
my head halfway between a nod and a shake, and the argument was over for that day. He asked after that merely
about the horses. I told him how they had each performed
during their workouts, and he seemed to forget that he
didn't believe I understood what I had seen. When I left
him, a short while later, he was again on the edge of sleep.

I rang the doorbell of my own flat in Hampstead, two
long and two short, and got three quick buzzes back,
which meant come on in. So I fitted my key into the latch
and opened the door.

Gillie's voice floated disembodiedly across the hall.

"I'm in your bedroom."

"Convenient," I said to myself with a smile. But she
was painting the walls.

"Didn't expect you tonight," she said when I kissed her.
She held her arms away from me, so as not to smear yellow ocher onto my jacket. There was a yellow streak on
her forehead and a dusting of it on her shining chestnut
hair and she looked companionable and easy. Gillie at
thirty-six had a figure no model would have been seen
dead in, and an attractive lived-in face with wisdom look-

ing out of gray-green eyes. She was sure and mature and much traveled in spirit, and had left behind her one collapsed marriage and one dead child. She had answered an advertisement for a tenant which I had put in the *Times*, and for two and a half years she had been my tenant and a lot else.

"What do you think of this color?" she said. "And we're having a cinnamon carpet and green and shocking-pink striped curtains."

"You can't mean it."

"It will look ravishing."

"Ugh," I said, but she simply laughed. When she had taken the flat, it had had white walls, polished furniture, and blue fabrics. Gillie had retained only the furniture, and Sheraton and Chippendale would have choked over their new settings.

"You look tired," she said. "Want some coffee?"

"And a sandwich, if there's any bread."

She thought. "There's some crisp bread, anyway."

She was permanently on diets, and her idea of dieting was not to buy food. This led to a lot of eating out, which completely defeated the object.

Gillie had listened attentively to my wise dictums about laying in suitable protein like eggs and cheese, and then continued happily in the same old ways, which brought me early on to believe that she really did not lust after a beauty-contest figure, but was content as long as she did not burst out of her forty-inch-hip dresses. Only when they got tight did she actually shed half a stone. She could if she wanted to. She didn't obsessively want to.

"How is your father?" she asked as I crunched my way through a sandwich of rye-crisp bread and slices of raw tomato.

"It's still hurting him."

"I would have thought they could have stopped that."

"Well, they do, most of the time. And the sister in charge told me this evening that he will be all right in a day or two. They aren't worried about his leg any more. The wound has started healing cleanly, and it should all be settling down soon and giving him an easier time."

"He's not young, of course."

"Sixty-seven," I agreed.

"The bones will take a fair time to mend."

"Mm."

"I suppose you've found someone to hold the fort."

"No," I said, "I'm staying there myself."

"Oh boy, oh boy," she said, "I might have guessed."

I looked at her inquiringly with my mouth full of bits.

"Anything which smells of challenge is your meat and drink."

"Not this one," I said with feeling.

"It will be unpopular with the stable," she diagnosed, "and apoplectic to your father, and riotous success."

"Correct on the first two, way out on the third."

She shook her head, with the glint of a smile. "Nothing is impossible for the whiz kids."

She knew I disliked the journalese term, and I knew she liked to use it. "My lover is a whiz kid," she said once into a hush at a sticky party; and the men mobbed her.

She poured me a glass of the marvelous Château Lafite 1961, which she sacrilegiously drank with anything from caviar to baked beans. It had seemed to me when she moved in that her belongings consisted almost entirely of fur coats and cases of wine, all of which she had precipitiously inherited from her mother and father respectively when they died together in Morocco in an earthquake. She had sold the coats, because she thought they made her look fat, and had set about drinking her way gradually through the precious bins that wine merchants were wringing their hands over.

"That wine is an *investment*," one of them had said to me in agony.

"But *someone's* got to drink it," said Gillie reasonably, and pulled out the cork on the second of the Cheval Blanc '61.

Gillie was so rich, because of her grandmother, that she found it more pleasing to drink the super-duper than to sell it at a profit and develop a taste for Brand X. She had been surprised that I had agreed, until I had pointed out that that flat was filled with precious pieces where painted deal would have done the same job. So we sat sometimes with our feet up on a sixteenth-century Spanish walnut refectory table which had brought dealers sobbing to their knees and drank her wine out of eighteenth-century

Waterford glass, and laughed at ourselves, because the only safe way to live with any degree of wealth was to make fun of it.

Gillie had said once, "I don't see why that table is so special, just because it's been here since the Armada. Just look at those moth-eaten legs." She pointed to four feet, which were pitted, stripped of polish, and worn untidily away.

"In the sixteenth century, they used to sluice the stone floors with beer because it whitened them," I said. "Beer was fine for the stone, but a bit unfortunate for any wood which got continually splashed."

"Rotten legs proves it's genuine?" she said.

"Got it in one."

I was fonder of that table than of anything else I possessed, because on it had been founded all my fortunes. Six months out of Eton, on what I had saved out of sweeping the floors at Sotheby's, I set up in business on my own pushing a barrow round the outskirts of flourishing country towns and buying anything worthwhile that I was offered. The junk I sold to secondhand shops and the best bits to dealers, and by the time I was seventeen I was thinking about a shop.

I saw the Spanish table in the garage of a handyman from whom I had just bought a late-Victorian chest of drawers. I looked at the wrought-iron crossed spars bracing the solid square legs under the four-inch-thick top, and felt unholy butterflies in my guts.

He had been using it as a trestle for paperhanging, and it was littered with pots of paint.

"I'll buy that, too, if you like," I said.

"It's only an old worktable."

"Well ... how much would you want for it?"

He looked at my barrow, onto which he had just helped me lift the chest of drawers. He looked at the twenty pounds I had paid him for it, and he looked at my shabby jeans and jerkin, and he said kindly, "No, lad, I couldn't rob you. And anyway, look, its legs are all rotten at the bottom."

"I could afford another twenty," I said doubtfully. "But that's about all I've got with me."

He took a lot of persuading, and in the end would only

let me give him fifteen. He shook his head over me, telling
me I'd better learn a bit more before I ruined myself. But
I cleaned up the table and repolished the beautiful slab of
walnut, and I sold it a fortnight later to a dealer I knew
from the Sotheby days for two hundred and seventy
pounds.

With those proceeds swelling my savings, I opened the
first shop, and things never looked back. When I sold out
twelve years later, to an American syndicate, there was a
chain of eleven stores, all bright and clean and filled with
treasures.

A short time afterward, on a sentimental urge, I traced
the Spanish table and bought it back. And I sought out
the handyman with his garage and gave him two hundred
pounds, which almost caused a heart attack; so I reckoned
if anyone was going to put his feet up on that expensive
plank, no one had a better right than I.

"Where did you get all those bruises?" Gillie said, sitting up in the spare-room bed and watching me undress.

I squinted down at the spatter of mauve blotches.

"I was attacked by a centipede."

She laughed. "You're hopeless."

"And I've got to be back at Newmarket by seven tomorrow morning."

"Stop wasting time, then. It's midnight already."

I climbed in beside her, lying together in naked com-
panionship we worked our way through the *Times* crossword.

It was always better like that. By the time we turned off
the light, we were relaxed and entwined, and we turned to
each other for an act that was a part but not the whole of
a relationship.

"I quite love you," Gillie said. "Believe it or not."

"Oh, I believe you," I said modestly. "Thousands
wouldn't."

"Stop biting my ear, I don't like it."

"The books say the ear is an A-1 erogenous zone."

"The books can go stuff themselves."

"Charming."

"And all those women's lib publications about 'The

Myth of the Vaginal Orgasm.' So much piffle. Of course it isn't a myth."

"This is not supposed to be a public meeting," I said. "This is supposed to be a spot of private passion."

"Oh, well . . . if you insist."

She wriggled more comfortably into my arms.

"I'll tell you something, if you like," she said.

"If you absolutely must."

"The answer to four down isn't hallucinated, it's hallucinogen."

I shook. "Thanks very much."

"Thought you'd like to know."

I kissed her neck and laid my hand on her stomach.

"That makes it a 'g,' not a 't,' in twenty across," she said.

"Stigma?"

"Clever old you."

"Is that the lot?"

"Mm."

After a bit, she said, "Do you really loathe the idea of green and shocking-pink curtains?"

"Would you mind just concentrating on the matter in hand?"

I could feel her grin in the darkness.

"O.K.," she said.

And concentrated.

She woke me up like an alarm clock at five o'clock. It was not so much the pat she woke me up with, but where she chose to plant it. I came back to the surface laughing.

"Good morning, little one," she said.

She got up and made some coffee, her chestnut hair in a tangle and her skin pale and fresh. She looked marvelous in the mornings. She stirred a dollop of heavy cream into the thick black coffee and sat opposite me across the kitchen table.

"Someone really had a go at you, didn't they?" she said casually.

I buttered a piece of rye crunch and reached for the honey.

"Sort of," I agreed.

"Not telling?"

"Can't," I said briefly. "But I will when I can."

"You may have a mind like teak," she said, "but you've a vulnerable body, just like anyone else."

I looked at her in surprise, with my mouth full. She wrinkled her nose at me.

"I used to think you mysterious and exciting," she said.

"Thanks."

"And now you're about as exciting as a pair of old bedroom slippers."

"So kind," I murmured.

"I used to think there was something magical about the way you disentangled all those nearly bankrupt businesses . . . and then I found out that it wasn't magic but just uncluttered common sense."

"Plain, boring old me," I agreed, washing down the crumbs with a gulp of coffee.

"I know you well now," she said. "I know how you tick. And all those bruises. . . ." She shivered suddenly in the warm little room.

"Gillie," I said accusingly, "you are suffering from intuition," and that remark in itself was a dead giveaway.

"No, from interpretation," she said. "And just you watch out for yourself."

"Anything you say."

"Because," she explained seriously, "I do not want to have the bother of hunting for another ground-floor flat with cellars to keep the wine in. It took me a whole month to find this one."

chapter 5

IT WAS drizzling when I got back to Newmarket. A cold wet horrible morning on the Heath. Also, the first thing I saw when I turned in to the drive of Rowley Lodge was the unwelcome white Mercedes.

The uniformed chauffeur sat behind the wheel. The steely young Alessandro sat in the back. When I stopped not far away from him, he was out of his car faster than I was out of mine.

"Where have you been?" he demanded, looking down his nose at my silver-gray Jensen.

"Where have you?" I said equably, and received a full freeze of the Rivera specialty in stares.

"I have come to begin," he said fiercely.

"So I see."

He wore superbly cut jodhpurs and glossy brown boots. His waterproof anorak had come from an expensive ski shop and his string gloves were clean and pale yellow. He looked more like an advertisement in *Country Life* than a working rider.

"I have to go in and change," I said. "You can begin when I come out."

"Very well."

He waited again in his car and emerged from it immediately I reappeared. I jerked my head at him to follow, and went down into the yard wondering just how much of a skirmish I was going to have with Etty.

She was in a box in bay three helping a very small lad to saddle a seventeen-hand filly, and with Alessandro at my heels I walked across to talk to her. She came out of the box and gave Alessandro a widening look of speculation.

"Etty," I said matter-of-factly, "this is Alessandro Rivera. He has signed his indentures. He starts today. Er, right now, in fact. What can we give him to ride?"

Etty cleared her throat. "Did you say *apprenticed?*"

"That's right."

"But we don't need any more lads," she protested.

"He won't be doing his two. Just riding exercise."

She gave me a bewildered look. "All apprentices do their two."

"Not this one," I said briskly. "How about a horse for him?"

She brought her scattered attention to bear on the immediate problem.

"There's Indigo," she said doubtfully. "I had him saddled for myself."

"Indigo will do beautifully." I nodded. Indigo was a quiet ten-year-old gelding which Etty often rode as lead horse to the two-year-olds, and upon which she liked to give completely untrained apprentices their first riding lessons. I stifled the urge to show Alessandro up by putting him on something really difficult; couldn't risk damaging expensive property.

"Miss Craig is the head lad," I told Alessandro. "And you will take your orders from her."

He gave her a black unfathomable stare, which she returned with uncertainty.

"I'll show him where Indigo is," I reassured her. "Also the tack room, and so on."

"I've given you Cloud Cuckoo-land this morning, Mr. Neil," she said hesitantly. "Jock will have got him ready."

"Fine," I said with a smile, but I didn't get one back.

I pointed out the tack room, feed room, and the general layout of the stable to Alessandro and led him back toward the drive.

"I do not take orders from a woman," he said.

"You'll have to," I said without emphasis.

"No."

"Goodbye, then."

He walked one pace behind me in fuming silence, but he followed me round to the outside boxes and did not peel off toward his car. Indigo's box was the one next to Moonrock's, and the horse stood patiently in his saddle and bridle, resting his weight on one leg and looking round lazily when I unbolted his door.

Alessandro's gaze swept him from stem to stern and he turned to me with unrepressed anger.

"I do not ride nags. I wish to ride Archangel."

"No one lets an apprentice diamond cutter start on the Kohinoor," I said.

"I can ride any race horse on earth. I can ride exceptionally well."

"Prove it on Indigo, then, and I'll give you something better for second lot."

He compressed his mouth. I looked at him with complete lack of feeling that always seemed to calm tempers in industrial negotiations, and after a moment or two it worked on him as well. His gaze dropped away from my face; he shrugged, untied Indigo's head-collar, and led him out of his box. He jumped with ease up into the saddle, slipped his feet into the stirrups, and gathered up the reins. His movements were precise and unfussy, and he settled onto old Indigo's back with an appearance of being at home. Without another word, he started walking away down the yard, shortening the stirrup leathers as he went, for Etty rode long.

Watching his back view, I followed him on foot, while from all the bays the lads led out the horses for the first lot. Down in the collecting paddock, they circled round the outer cinder track while Etty, on the grass in the center, began the ten-minute task of swapping some of the riders. The lads who did the horses did not necessarily ride their own charges out at exercise; each horse had to be ridden by a rider who could at the least control him and at the most improve him. The lowliest riders usually got the task of walking any unfit horses round the paddock at home; Etty seldom let them loose in canters on the Heath.

I joined her in the center as she referred to her list. She was wearing a bright yellow sou'wester down which the drizzle trickled steadily, and she looked like a diminutive American fisherman. The scrawled list in her hand was slowly degenerating into pulp.

"Ginge, get up on Pulitzer," she said.

Ginge did as he was told in a sulk. Pulitzer was a far cry from Lucky Lindsay, and he considered that he had lost face.

Etty briefly watched Alessandro plod round on Indigo, taking in with a flick of a glance that he could at least manage him with no problems. She looked at me in a baffled questioning way, but I merely steered her away from

him by asking who she was putting up on our problem
colt, Traffic.

She shook her head in frustration. "It'll still have to be
Andy. . . . He's a right little devil, that Traffic. All that
breed, you can't trust one of them." She turned and called
on him "Andy, get up on Traffic."

Andy, middle-aged, tiny, wrinkled, could ride the
sweetest of training gallops; but my father had mentioned
that when, years before, Andy had been given his chance
in races, his wits had flown out of the window, and his
grasp of tactics was nil. He was given a leg up onto the
dark irritable two-year-old, which jigged and fidgeted and
buck-jumped under him without remission.

Etty had switched herself to Lucky Lindsay, who wore
a shield over the cut knee and, although sound, would not
be cantering; in Cloud Cuckoo-land she had given me the
next best to a hack, a strong five-year-old handicapper up
to a man's weight. With everyone mounted, the gates to
the Heath were opened, and the whole string wound out
onto the walking ground, colts as always in front, fillies
behind.

Bound for the Southfield Gallops beside the racecourse,
we turned right out of the gate and walked down behind
the other stables which were strung out along the Bury
Road. Passed the Jockey Club notice board announcing
which training areas could be used that day. Crossed the
A 11, holding up heavy lorries with their windscreen
wipers twitching impatiently. Wound across the Severalls,
along the Watercourse, through St. Mary's Square, along
the Rows, and so finally to Southfields. No other town in
England provided a special series of roads upon which the
only traffic allowed was horses; but one could go from one
end of Newmarket to the other, only yards behind its bus-
tling High Street, and spend just a fraction of the journey
on the public highway.

We were the only string on Southfields that morning,
and Etty wasted no time in starting the canters. Up on the
road to the racecourse stood the two usual cars, with two
men standing out in the damp in the unmistakable position which meant they were watching us through binoculars.

"They never miss a day," Etty said sourly. "And if they

think we've brought Archangel down here, they're in for a disappointment."

The touts watched steadfastly, though what they could see from half a mile away through unrelenting drizzle was anyone's guess. They were employed not by bookmakers but by racing columnists, who relied on their reports for the wherewithal to fill their pages. I thought it might be a very good thing if I could keep Alessandro out of their attention for as long as possible.

He could handle Indigo right enough, though the gelding was an undemanding old thing within the powers of the Pony Club. All the same, he sat well on him and had quiet hands. "Here, you," Etty said, beckoning to him with her whip. "Come over here."

To me she said, as she slid to the ground from Lucky Lindsay, "What is his name?"

"Alessandro."

"Aless—? Far too long."

Indigo was reined to a halt beside her. "You, Alex," she said. "Jump down and hold this horse."

I thought he would explode. His furious face said plainly that no one had any right to call him Alex, and that no one, but no one, was going to order him about. Especially not a woman.

He saw me watching him and suddenly wiped all expression from his own face as if with a sponge. He shook his feet out of the irons, swung his leg agilely forward over Indigo's withers, and slid to the ground facing us. He took the reins of Lucky Lindsay, which Etty held out to him, and gave her those of Indigo. She lengthened the stirrup leathers, climbed up into the saddle, and rode away without comment to give a lead to the six two-year-olds we had brought with us.

Alessandro said, like a throttled volcano, "I am not going to take any more orders from that woman."

"Don't be so bloody silly," I said.

He looked up at me. The fine rain had drenched his black hair so that the curls had tightened and clung close to his head. With the arrogant nose, the back-tilted skull, the close-curling hair, he looked like a Roman statue come to life.

"Don't talk to me like that. No one talks to me like that."

Cloud Cuckoo-land stood patiently, pricking his ears up to watch some sea gulls fly across the Heath.

I said, "You are here because you want to be. No one asked you to come, no one will stop you going. But just so long as you do stay here, you will do what Miss Craig says, and you will do what I say, and you will do it without arguing. Is that clear?"

"My father will not let you treat me like this." He was rigid with the strength of his outrage.

"Your father," I said coldly, "must be overjoyed to have a son who needs to shelter behind his skirts."

"You will be sorry," he threatened furiously.

I shrugged. "Your father said I was to give you good horses to ride in races. Nothing was mentioned about bowing down to a spoiled little tin god."

"I will tell him—"

"Tell him what you like. But the more you run to him, the less I'll think of you."

"I don't care what you think of me," he said vehemently.

"You're a liar," I said flatly, and he gave me a long tight-lipped stare until he turned abruptly away. He led Lucky Lindsay ten paces off, and stopped and watched the canters that Etty was directing. Every line of the slender shape spoke of injured pride and flaming resentment, and I wondered whether his father would indeed think that I had gone too far. And if I had, what was he going to do about it?

Mentally shrugging off the evil until the day thereof, I tried to make some assessment of the two-year-olds' relative abilities. Scoff as people might about me taking over my father's license, I had found that childhood skills came back after nineteen years as naturally as riding a bicycle; and few lonely children could grow up in a racing stable without learning the trade from the muckheap up. I'd had the horses out-of-doors for company, and the furniture indoors, and I reckoned if I could build one business out of the deadwood I could also try to keep things rolling with the live muscles. But for only as long, I reminded myself, as it took me to get rid of Alessandro.

Etty came back after the canters and changed horses again.

"Give me a leg up," she said briskly to Alessandro; for Lucky Lindsay like most young thoroughbreds did not like riders climbing up to mount them.

For a moment, I thought the whole pantomime was over. Alessandro drew himself up to his full height, which topped Etty's by at least two inches, and dispatched at her a glare which should have cremated her. Etty genuinely didn't notice.

"Come on," she said impatiently, and held out her leg backward, bent at the knee.

Alessandro threw a glance of desperation in my direction, then took a visibly deep breath, looped Indigo's reins over his arm, and put his two hands under Etty's shin. He gave her quite a respectable leg up, though I wouldn't have been surprised if it was the first time in his life that he had done it.

I carefully didn't laugh, didn't sneer, didn't show that I thought there was anything to notice. Alessandro swallowed his capitulation in private. But there was nothing to indicate that it would be permanent.

We rode back in the rain through the town and into the yard, where I gave Cloud Cuckoo-land back to Jock and walked into the office to see Margaret. She had the mushroom heater blowing full blast, but I doubted that I would have properly dried through by the time we pulled out again for second lot.

"Morning," she said economically.

I nodded, half smiled, slouched into the swivel chair. "I've opened the letters again—was that right?" she said.

"Absolutely. And answer them yourself, if you can."

She looked surprised. "Mr. Griffon always dictates everything."

"Anything you have to ask about, ask. Anything I need to know, tell me. Anything else, deal with it yourself."

"All right," she said, and sounded pleased.

I sat in my father's chair and stared down at his books, which I had usurped, and thought seriously about what I had seen in his account books. Alessandro wasn't the only trouble the stable was running into.

There was a sudden crash as the door from the yard

was forcibly opened, and Etty burst into the office like a stampeding ballistic missile.

"That bloody boy you've taken on— He'll have to go. I'm not standing for it. I'm not."

She looked extremely annoyed, with eyes blinking fiercely and her mouth pinched into a slit.

"What has he done?" I asked resignedly.

"He's gone off in that stupid white car and left Indigo in his box still with his saddle and bridle on. George says he just got down off Indigo, led him into the box, and came out and shut the door, and got into the car and the chauffeur drove him away. Just like that!" She paused for breath. "And who does he think is going to take the saddle off and dry the rain off Indigo and wash out his feet and rug him up and fetch his hay and water and make his bed?"

"I'll go out and see George," I said. "And ask him to do it."

"I've asked him already," Etty said furiously. "But that's not the point. We're not keeping that wretched little Alex. Not one more minute."

She glanced at me with her chin up, making an issue of it. Like all head lads, she had a major say in the hiring and firing of the help. I had not consulted her over the hiring of Alessandro, and clear as a bell she was telegraphing that I was to acknowledge her authority and get rid of him.

"I'm afraid that we'll have to put up with him, Etty," I said sympathetically. "And hope to teach him better ways."

"He must go," she insisted vehemently.

"Alessandro's father," I lied sincerely, "is paying through the nose to have his son taken on here as an apprentice. It is very much worth the stable's while financially to put up with him. I'll have a talk with him when he comes back for second lot and see if I can get him to be more reasonable."

"I don't like the way he stares at me," Etty said, unmollified.

"I'll ask him not to."

"Ask!" Etty said exasperatedly. "Whoever heard of

asking an apprentice to behave with respect to the head lad!"

"I'll tell him," I said.

"And tell him to stop being so snooty with the other lads—they are already complaining. And tell him he is to put his horse straight after he has ridden it, the same as all the others."

"I'm sorry, Etty. I don't think he'll put his horse straight. We'll have to get George to do it regularly. For a bonus, of course."

Etty said angrily, "It's not a yard man's job to act as a—a—*servant*—to an *apprentice*. It just isn't right."

"I know, Etty," I said. "I know it isn't right. But Alessandro is not an ordinary apprentice, and it might be easier all round if you could let all the other lads know that his father is paying for him to be here, and that he has some romantic notion of wanting to be a jockey, which he'll get out of his system soon enough, and when he has gone, we call all get back to normal."

She looked at me uncertainly. "It isn't a proper apprenticeship if he doesn't look after his horses."

"The details of an apprenticeship are a matter for agreement between the contracting parties," I said regretfully. "If I agree that he doesn't have to do his two, then he doesn't have to. And I don't really approve of him not doing them, but there you are, the stable will be richer if he doesn't."

Etty had calmed down but she was not pleased. "I think you might have consulted me before agreeing to all this."

"Yes, Etty. I'm very sorry."

"And does your father know about it?"

"Of course," I said.

"Oh, well, then." She shrugged. "If your father wants it, I suppose we must make the best of it. But it won't be at all good for discipline."

"The lads will be used to him within a week."

"They won't like it if he looks like getting any chance in races which they think should be theirs."

"The season doesn't start for a month," I said soothingly. "Let's see how he makes out, shall we?"

And put off the day when he got the chances however

bad he was, and however much they should have gone to
someone else.

Etty put him on a quiet four-year-old mare which
didn't please him but was a decided step up from old Indigo. He had received with unyielding scorn my request
that he should stop staring so disquietingly at Etty, and
sneered at my suggestion that he should let it be understood that his father was paying for him to be there.

"It is not true," he said superciliously.

"Believe me," I said with feeling, "if it were true, you
wouldn't be here tomorrow. Not if he paid a pound a
minute."

"Why not?"

"Because you are upsetting Miss Craig and upsetting
the other lads, and a stable seething with resentment is not
going to do its best by its horses. In fact, if you want the
horses here to win races for you, you'll do your best to get
along without arousing ill feeling in the staff."

He had given me the black stare and hadn't answered,
but I noticed that he looked steadfastly at the ground
when Etty detailed him to the mare. He rode her quietly
along toward the back of the string and completed his allotted half-speed four-furlong canter without incident. On
our return to the yard, George met him and took the mare
away to the box, and Alessandro without a backward
glance walked into his Mercedes and was driven away.

The truce lasted for two more mornings. On each of
them, Alessandro arrived punctually for the first exercise,
disappeared presumably for breakfast, came back for the
second lot, and departed for the rest of the day. Etty gave
him middling horses to ride, all of which he did ade-
quately enough to wring from her the grudging comment
"If he doesn't give us any more trouble, I suppose it could
be worse."

But on his fourth morning, which was Saturday, the
defiant attitude was not only back but reinforced. We survived through both lots without a direct confrontation between him and Etty only because I purposely kept parting
them. For the second lot, in fact, I insisted on taking him
with me and a party of two-year-olds along to the special

two-year-old training ground while Etty led the bulk of the string over to Warren Hill.

We got back before Etty so that he should be gone before she returned, but instead of striding away to his Mercedes he followed me to the office door.

"Griffon," he said behind me.

I turned, regarded him. The arrogant stare was much in evidence. His eyes were blacker than space.

"I have been to see my father," he said. "He says that you should be treating me with deference. He says I should not take orders from a woman and that you must arrange that I do not. If necessary, Miss Craig must leave. He says I must be given better horses to ride, and in particular, Archangel. He says that if you do not see to these things immediately, he will show you that he meant what he said. And he told me to give you this. He said it was a promise of what he could do."

He produced a flat tin box from an inner pocket of his anorak, and held it out to me.

I took it. I said, "Do you know what it contains?"

He shook his head, but I was sure he did know.

"Alessandro," I said, "whatever your father threatens, or whatever he does, your only chance of success is to leave the stable unharmed. If your father destroys it, there will be nothing for you to ride."

"He will make another trainer take me," he asserted.

"He will not," I said flatly, "because should he destroy this stable I will put all the facts in front of the Jockey Club and they will take away your license and stop you riding in any races whatsoever."

"He would kill you," he said matter-of-factly. The thought of it did not surprise or appall him.

"I have already lodged with my solicitor a full account of my interview with your father. Should he kill me, they will open that letter. He could find himself in great trouble. And you, of course, would be barred for life from racing anywhere in the world."

A lot of the starch had turned to frustration. "He will have to talk to you himself," he said. "You do not behave as he tells me you will. You confuse me. He will talk to you himself."

He turned on his heel and took himself stiffly away to

the attendant Mercedes. He climbed into the back, and
the patient chauffeur, who always waited in the car all the
time that his passenger was on the horses, started the
purring engine and, with a scrunch of his Michelins, carried him away.

I took the flat tin with me into the house, through into
the oak-paneled room, and opened it there on the desk.

Between layers of cotton wool, it contained a small
carved wooden model of a horse. Round its neck was tied
a label, and on the label was written one word: "Moonrock."

I picked the little horse out of the tin. It was necessary
to lift it out in two pieces, because the off-hind leg was
snapped through at the hock.

chapter 6

I SAT for quite a long time turning the little model over in my hands, and its significance over in my mind, wondering whether Enso Rivera could possibly have organized the breaking of Moonrock's leg, or whether he was simply pretending that what had been a true accident was all his own work.

I did not on the whole believe that he had destroyed Moonrock. What did become instantly ominous, though, was his repeated choice of the word "destroy."

Almost every horse which broke a leg had to be destroyed, as only in exceptional cases was mending them practicable. Horses could not be kept in bed. They would scarcely ever even lie down. To take a horse's weight off a leg meant supporting him in slings. Supporting him in slings for the number of weeks that it took a major bone to mend incurred debility and gut troubles. Race horses, always delicate creatures, could die of the inactivity, and if they survived were never as good afterward; and only in the case of valuable stallions and brood mares was any attempt normally made to keep them alive.

If Enso Rivera broke a horse's leg, it would have to be destroyed. If he broke enough of them, the owners would remove their survivors in a panic, and the stable itself would be destroyed.

Alessandro had said his father had sent the tin as a promise of what he could do.

If he could break horses' legs, he could indeed destroy the stable.

But it wasn't as easy as all that to break a horse's leg.

Fact or bluff.

I fingered the little maimed horse. I didn't know, and couldn't decide, which it represented. But I did decide at least to turn a bit of my own bluff into fact.

I wrote a full account of the abduction, embellished with every detail I could remember. I packed the little wooden horse back into its tin and wrote a short explanation of its possible significance. Then I enclosed everything in a strong manila envelope, wrote on it the time-honored words "To be opened in the event of my death," put it into a larger envelope with a covering letter, and posted it to my London solicitor from the main post office in Newmarket.

"You've done *what?*" my father exclaimed.

"Taken on a new apprentice."

He looked in fury at all the junk anchoring him to his bed. Only the fact that he was tied down prevented him from hitting the ceiling.

"It isn't up to you to take on new apprentices. You are not to do it. Do you hear?"

I repeated my fabrication about Enso paying well for Alessandro's privilege. The news percolated through my father's irritation and the voltage went out of it perceptibly. A thoughtful expression took over, and finally a grudging nod.

He knows, I thought. He knows that the stable will before long be short of ready cash.

I wondered whether he was well enough to discuss it, or whether, even if he was well enough, he would be able to talk to me about it. We had never in our lives discussed anything; he had told me what to do, and I either had or hadn't done it. The divine right of kings had nothing on his attitude, which he applied also to most of the owners. They were all in varying degrees in awe of him and a few were downright afraid; but they kept their horses in his stable because year after year he brought home the races that counted.

He asked how the horses were working. I told him at some length, and he listened with a skeptical slant to his mouth and eyebrows, intending to show doubt of the worth of any or all of my assessments. I continued without rancor through everything of any interest, and at the end he said, "Tell Etty I want a list of the work done by each horse, and its progress."

"All right," I agreed readily. He searched my face for signs of resentment and seemed a shade disappointed when he didn't find any. The antagonism of an aging and infirm father toward a fully grown healthy son was a fairly universal manifestation throughout nature, and I wasn't fussed that he was showing it. But all the same I was not going to give him the satisfaction of feeling he had scored over me; and he had no idea of how practiced I was at taking the prideful flush out of people's ill-natured victories.

I said merely, "Shall I take a list of the entries home, so that Etty will know which races the horses are to be prepared for?"

His eyes narrowed and his mouth tightened, and he explained that it had been impossible for him to do the entries; treatment and X-rays took up so much of his time and he was not left alone long enough to concentrate.

"Shall Etty and I have a go, between us?"

"Certainly not. I will do them ... when I have more time."

"All right," I said. "How is the leg feeling? You are certainly looking more your own self now."

"It is less troublesome," he admitted. He smoothed the already wrinkle-free bedclothes which lay over his stomach, engaged in his perennial habit of making his surroundings as orderly, as dignified, as starched as his soul.

I asked if there was anything I could bring him. "A book," I suggested. "Or some fruit? Or some champagne?" Like most race-horse trainers, he saw champagne as a sort of superior Coca-Cola, best drunk in the mornings if at all, but he knew that as a pick-me-up for the sick it had few equals.

He inclined his head sidewise, considering. "There are some half bottles in the cellar at Rowley Lodge."

"I'll bring some," I said.

He nodded. He would never, whatever I did, say thank you. I smiled inwardly. The day my father thanked me would be the day his personality disintegrated.

Via the hospital telephone, I checked whether I would be welcome at Hampstead and, having received a warming affirmative, headed the Jensen along the eight miles further south.

Gillie had finished painting the bedroom, but its furniture was still stacked in the hall.

"Waiting for the carpet," she explained. "Like Godot."

"Godot never came," I commented.

"That," she agreed with exaggerated patience, "is what I mean."

"Send up rockets, then."

"Firecrackers have been going off under backsides since Tuesday."

"Never mind," I said soothingly. "Come out to dinner."

"I'm on a grapefruit day," she objected.

"Well, I'm not. Positively not. I had no lunch and I'm hungry."

"I've got a really awfully nice grapefruit recipe. You put the halves in the oven doused in saccharin and kirsch and eat it hot. . . ."

"No," I said definitely. "I'm going to the Empress."

That shattered the grapefruit program. She adored the Empress.

"Oh, well . . . it would be so boring for you to eat alone," she said. "Wait a mo while I put on my tatty black."

Her tatty black was a long-sleeved St. Laurent dress that made the least of her curves. There was nothing approaching tatty about it, very much on the contrary, and her description was inverted, as if by diminishing its standing she could forget her guilt over its price. She had recently developed some vaguely Socialist views, and it had mildly begun to bother her that what she had paid for one dress would have supported a ten-child family throughout Lent.

Dinner at the Empress was its usual quiet, spacious, superb self. Gillie ordered curried prawns to be followed by chicken in a cream-and-brandy sauce, and laughed when she caught my ironic eye.

"Back to the grapefruit," she agreed. "But not until tomorrow."

"How are the suffering orphans?" I asked. She worked three days a week for an adoption society which, because of the Pill and easy abortion, was running out of its raw materials.

"You don't happen to want two-year-old twins, Afro-Asian boys, one of them with a squint?" she said.

"Not all that much, no."

"Poor little things." She absent-mindedly ate a bread

roll spread with enjoyable chunks of butter. "We'll never place them. They don't look even averagely attractive."

"Squints can be put right," I said.

"Someone has to care enough first, to get it done."

We drank a lesser wine than Gillie's but better than most.

"Do you realize," Gillie said, "that a family of ten could live for a week on what this dinner is costing?"

"Perhaps the waiter has a family of ten," I suggested. "And if we didn't eat it, what would they live on?"

"Oh . . . blah," Gillie said, but looked speculatively at the man who brought her chicken.

She asked how my father was. I said better, but by no means well.

"He said he would do the entries," I explained, "but he hasn't started. He told me it was because he isn't given time, but the sister says he sleeps a great deal. He had a frightful shaking and his system hasn't recovered yet."

"What will you do, then, about the entries? Wait until he's better?"

"Can't. The next lot have to be in by Wednesday."

"What happens if they aren't?"

"The horses will go on eating their heads off in the stable when they ought to be out on a racecourse trying to earn their keep. It's now or never to put their names down for some of the races at Chester and Ascot and the Craven meeting at Newmarket."

"So you'll do them yourself," she said matter-of-factly. "And they'll all go and win."

"Almost any entry is better than no entry at all." I sighed. "And by the law of averages, some of them must be right."

"There you are, then. No more problems."

But there were two more problems, and worse ones, sticking up like rocks on the fairway. The financial problem, which I could solve if I had to; and that of Alessandro, which I didn't yet know how to.

The following morning, he arrived late. The horses for first lot were already plodding round the cinder track, while I stood with Etty in the center as she changed the riders, when Alessandro appeared through the gate from the yard. He waited for a space between the passing horses and then crossed the cinder track and came toward us.

The finery of the week before was undimmed. The boots shone as glossily, the gloves as palely, and the ski jacket and jodhpurs were still immaculate. On his head, however, he wore a blue-and-white striped woolly cap with a pompon, the same as most of the other lads; but on Alessandro this cozy protection against the stinging March wind looked as incongruous as a bowler hat on the beach.

I didn't even smile. The black eyes regarded me with their customary chill from features that were more gaunt than delicate. The strong shape of the bones showed clearly through the yellowish skin, and more so, it seemed to me, than a week ago.

"What do you weigh?" I asked abruptly.

He hesitated a little. "I will be able to ride at six stone seven when the races begin. I will be able to claim all the allowances."

"But now? What do you weigh now?"

"A few pounds more. But I will lose them."

Etty fumed at him but forbore to point out to him that he wouldn't get any rides if he wasn't good enough. She looked down at her list to see which horses she had allotted him, opened her mouth to tell him, and then shut it again, and I literally saw the impulse take hold of her.

"Ride Traffic," she said. "You can get up on Traffic."

Alessandro stood very still.

"He doesn't have to," I said to Etty; and to Alessandro, "You don't have to ride Traffic. Only if you choose."

He swallowed. He raised his chin and his courage, and said, "I choose."

With a stubborn set to her mouth, Etty beckoned to Andy, who was already mounted on Traffic, and told him of the change.

"Happy to oblige," Andy said feelingly, and gave Alessandro a leg up into his unrestful place. Traffic lashed out into a few preliminary bucks, found he had a less hard-bitten customer than usual on his back, and started off at a rapid sidewise trot across the paddock.

Alessandro didn't fall off, which was the best that could be said. He hadn't the experience to settle the sour colt to obedience, let alone to teach him to be better, but he was managing a great deal more efficiently than I could have done.

Etty watched him with disfavor and told everyone to give him plenty of room.

"That nasty little squirt needs taking down a peg," she said in unnecessary explanation.

"He isn't doing too badly," I commented.

"Huh." There was a ten-ton lorry-load of scorn in her voice. "Look at the way he's jabbing him in the mouth. You wouldn't catch Andy doing that in a thousand years."

"Better not let him out on the Heath," I said.

"Teach him a lesson," Etty said doggedly.

"Might kill the goose, and then where would we be for the golden eggs?"

She gave me a bitter glance. "The stable doesn't need that sort of money."

"The stable needs any sort of money it can get."

But Etty shook her head in disbelief. Rowley Lodge had been in the top division of the big league ever since she had joined it, and no one would ever convince her that its very success was leading it into trouble.

I beckoned to Alessandro and he came as near as his rocking horse permitted.

"You don't have to ride him on the Heath," I said.

Traffic turned his quarters toward us and Alessandro called over his shoulder, "I stay here. I choose."

Etty told him to ride fourth in the string and everyone else to keep out of his way. She herself climbed into Indigo's saddle, and I into Cloud Cuckoo-land's, and George opened the gates. We turned right onto the walking ground, bound for the canter on Warren Hill, and nothing frantic happened on the way except that Traffic practically backed into an incautious tout when crossing Moulton Road. The tout retreated with curses, calling the horse by name. The Newmarket touts knew every horse on the Heath by sight. A remarkable feat, as there were about two thousand animals in training there, hundreds of them two-year-olds which altered shape as they developed month by month. Touts learned horses as headmasters learned new boys, and rarely made a mistake. All I hoped was that this one had been too busy getting himself to safety to take much notice of the rider.

We had to wait our turn on Warren Hill, since we were the fourth stable to choose to work there that morning. Alessandro walked Traffic round in circles a little way apart—or at least tried to walk him. Traffic's idea of walking would have tired a bucking bronco.

Eventually, Etty sent the string off up the hill in small clusters, with me sitting halfway up the slope on Cloud Cuckoo-land, watching them as they swept past. At the top of the hill, they stopped, peeled off to the left, and went back down the central walking ground to collect again at the bottom. Most mornings each horse cantered up the hill twice, the sharpish incline getting a lot of work into them in a comparatively short distance.

Alessandro started up the hill in the last bunch, one of only four.

Long before he drew level with me, I could see that of the horse and rider it was the horse who had control. Galloping was hard labor up Warren Hill, but no one had given Traffic the message.

As he passed me, he was showing all the classic signs of the bolter in action: head stretched horizontally forward, bit gripped between his teeth, eyes showing the whites. Alessandro, with as much hope of dominating the situation as a virgin in a troopship, hung grimly on to the neck strap and appeared to be praying.

The top of the rise meant nothing to Traffic. He swerved violently to the left and set off sidewise toward Bury Hill, not even having the sense to make straight for the stable but swinging too far north and missing it by half a mile. On he charged, his hoofs thundering relentlessly over the turf, carrying Alessandro inexorably away in the general direction of Lowestoft.

Stifling the unworthy thought that I wouldn't care all that much if he plunged straight on into the North Sea, I reflected with a bit more sense that if Traffic damaged himself, Rowley Lodge's foundations would feel the tremor. I set off at a trot after him as he disappeared into the distance, but when I reached the Bury St. Edmunds Road there was no sign of him. I crossed the road and reined in there, wondering which direction to take.

A car came slowly toward me with a shocked-looking driver poking his head out of the window.

"Some bloody madman nearly plowed straight into me," he yelled. "Some bloody madman on the road on a mad horse."

"How very upsetting," I shouted back sympathetically, but he glared at me balefully and nearly ran into a tree.

I went on along the road, wondering whether it would be a dumped-off Alessandro I saw first, and if so, how long it would take to find and retrieve the wayward Traffic.

From the next rise, there was no sign of either of them; the road stretched emptily ahead. Beginning to get anxious, I quickened Cloud Cuckoo-land until we were trotting fast along the soft ground edging the tarmac.

Past the end of the Limekilns, still no trace of Alessandro. The road ran straight, up and down its inclines. No Alessandro. It was a good two miles from the training ground that I finally found him.

He was standing at the crossroads, dismounted, holding Traffic's reins. The colt had evidently run himself to a standstill, as he drooped there with his head down, his sides heaving, and sweat streaming from him all over. Flecks of foam spattered his neck, and his tongue lolled exhaustedly out.

I slid down from Cloud Cuckoo-land and ran my hand down Traffic's legs. No tenderness. No apparent strain. Sighing with relief, I straightened up and looked at Alessandro. His face was stiff, his eyes expressionless.

"Are you all right?" I asked.

He lifted his chin. "Of course."

"He's a difficult horse," I remarked.

Alessandro didn't answer. His self-pride might have received a body blow, but he was not going to be so soft as to accept any comfort.

"You'd better walk back with him," I said. "Walk until he's thoroughly cooled down. And keep him out of the way of the cars."

Alessandro tugged the reins and Traffic sluggishly turned, not moving his legs until he absolutely had to.

"What's that?" Alessandro said, pointing to a mound in the grass at the corner of the crossroads where he had been standing. He shoved Traffic farther away so that I could see; but I had no need to.

"It's the Boy's Grave," I said.

"What boy?" He was startled. The small grave was known to everyone in Newmarket, but not to him. The mound, about four feet long, was outlined with overlapping wire hoops, like the edges of lawns in parks. There were some dirty-looking plastic daffodils entwined in the hoops, and a few dying flowers scattered in the center. Also a white plastic drinking mug which someone had thrown there. The grave looked forlorn yet, in a futile sort of way, cared for.

"There are a lot of legends," I said. "The most likely is that he was a shepherd boy who went to sleep in charge of his flock. A wolf came and killed half of them, and when he woke up he was so remorseful that he hanged himself."

"They used to bury suicides at crossroads," Alessandro said, nodding. "It is well known."

There didn't seem to be any harm in trying to humanize him, so I went on with the story.

"The grave is always looked after, in a haphazard sort of way. It is never overgrown, and fresh flowers are often put there. No one knows exactly who puts them there, but it's supposed to be the gypsies. And there is also a legend that in May the flowers on the grave are in the colors that will win the Derby."

Alessandro stared down at the pathetic little memorial.

"There are no black flowers," he said slowly: Archangel's colors were black, pale blue, and gold.

"The gypsies will solve that if they have to," I said dryly, and thought that they would opt for an easier nap selection.

I turned Cloud Cuckoo-land in the direction of home and walked away. When presently I looked back, Alessandro was walking Traffic quietly along the side of the road, a thin straight figure in his clean clothes and bright blue-and-white cap. It was a pity, I thought, that he was as he was. With a different father, he might have been a different person.

But with a different father, so would I. And who wouldn't.

I thought about it all the way back to Rowley Lodge.

Fathers, it seemed to me, could train, feed, or warp their young plants, but they couldn't affect their basic nature. They might produce a stunted oak or a luxuriant weed, but oak and weed were inborn qualities, which would prevail in the end. Alessandro, on such a horticultural reckoning, was like a cross between holly and deadly nightshade; and if his father had his way the red berries would lose out to the black.

Alessandro bore Etty's strongly implied scorn with a frozen face, but few of the other lads teased him on his return, as they would have done to one of their own sort. Most of them seemed to be instinctively afraid of him, which to my mind showed their good sense, and the other, less sensitive types had drifted into the defense mechanism of ignoring his existence.

George took Traffic off to his box, and Alessandro followed me into the office. His glance swept over Margaret, sitting at her desk in a neat navy-blue dress with the high curls piled as elaborately as ever, but he saw her as no bar to giving me the benefit of the thoughts that he evidently had also had time for on the way back.

"You should not have made me ride such a badly trained horse," he began belligerently.

"I didn't make you. You chose to."

"Miss Craig told me to ride it to make a fool of me."

True enough.

"You could have refused," I said.

"I could not."

"You could have said that you thought you needed more practice before taking on the worst ride in the yard."

His nostrils flared. So self-effacing an admission would have been beyond him.

"Anyway," I went on, "I personally don't think riding Traffic is going to teach you much. So you won't be put on him again."

"But I insist," he said vehemently.

"You insist what?"

"I insist I ride Traffic again." He gave me the haughtiest of his selection of stares, and added, "Tomorrow."

"Why?"

"Because if I do not, everyone will think it is because I cannot, or that I am afraid to."

"So you do care what the others think of you," I said matter-of-factly.

"No, I do not." He denied it strongly.

"Then why ride the horse?"

He compressed his strong mouth stubbornly. "I will answer no more questions. I will ride Traffic tomorrow."

"Well, O.K.," I said casually. "But I'm not sending him on the Heath tomorrow. He'll hardly need another canter. Tomorrow he'll only be walking round the cinder track in the paddock, which will be very boring for you."

He gave me a concentrated, suspicious, considering stare, trying to work out if I was meaning to undermine him. Which I was, if one can call taking the point out of a Grand Gesture undermining.

"Very well," he said grudgingly. "I will ride him round the paddock."

He turned on his heel and walked out of the office. Margaret watched him go with a mixed expression I couldn't read.

"Mr. Griffon would never stand for him talking like that," she said.

"Mr. Griffon doesn't have to."

"I can see why Etty can't bear him," she said. "He's insolent. There's no other word for it. Insolent." She handed me three opened letters across the desk. "These need your attention, if you don't mind." She reverted to Alessandro: "But all the same, he's beautiful."

"He's no such thing," I protested mildly. "If anything, he's ugly."

She smiled briefly. "He's absolutely loaded with sex appeal."

I lowered the letters. "Don't be silly. He has the sex appeal of a bag of rusty nails."

"You wouldn't notice," she said judiciously. "Being a man."

I shook my head. "He's only eighteen."

"Age has nothing to do with it," she said. "Either you've got it, or you haven't got it, right from the start. And he's got it."

I didn't pay much attention; Margaret herself had so

little sex appeal that I didn't think her a reliable judge.
When I'd read through the letters and agreed with her
how she should answer them, I went along to the kitchen
for some coffee.

The remains of the night's work lay littered about: the
various dregs of brandy, cold milk, coffee, and masses of
scribbled-on bits of paper. It had taken me most of the
night to do the entries, a night I would far rather have
spent lying warmly in Gillie's bed.

The entries had been difficult, not only because I had
never done them before, and had to read the conditions of
each race several times to make sure I understood them,
but also because of Alessandro. I had to make a balance
of what I would have done without him and what I would
have to let him ride if he was still there in a month's time.

I was continuing to take his father's threats seriously.
Part of the time, I thought I was foolish to do so; but that
abduction a week ago had been no playful joke, and until
I was certain Enso would not let loose a thunderbolt it
was more prudent to go along with his son. I still had
nearly a month before the Flat season started, still nearly a
month to see a quick way out. But, just in case, I had put
down some of the better prospects for apprentice races,
and had duplicated the entries in many open races, because if two ran there would be one for Alessandro. Also
I entered a good many in the lesser meetings, particularly
those in the north; whether he liked it or not, Alessandro
was not going to start his career in a blaze of limelight.
After all that, I dug around in the office until I found the
book in which old Robinson had recorded all the previous
years' entries, and I checked my provisional list against
what my father had done. After subtracting about twenty
names, because I had been much too lavish, and shuffling
things around a little, I made the total number of entries
for the week approximately the same as those for the year
before, except that I still had more in the north. Then I
wrote the final list onto the official yellow form, in block
letters as requested, and double-checked again to make
sure I hadn't entered two-year-olds in handicaps, or fillies
in colts-only, and made any other such giveaway gaffes.

When I gave the completed form to Margaret to record

and then post, all she said was "This isn't your father's writing."

"No," I said. "He dictated the entries. I wrote them down."

She nodded noncommittally, and whether she believed me or not I had no idea.

Alessandro rode Pulitzer competently next day at first lot, and kept himself to himself. After breakfast he returned with a stony face that forbade comment, and when the main string had started out onto the Heath, was given a leg up onto Traffic. Looking back from the gate, I saw the fractious colt kicking away at shadows, as usual, and noticed that the two other lads detailed to stay in and walk their charges were keeping well away from him.

When we returned an hour and a quarter later, George was holding Traffic's reins, the other lads had dismounted, and Alessandro was lying on the ground in an unconscious heap.

chapter 7

"TRAFFIC JUST bucked him off, sir," one of the lads said. "Just bucked him clean off, sir. And he hit his head on the paddock rail, sir."

"Just this minute, sir," added the other anxiously.

They were both about sixteen, both apprentices, both tiny, neither of them very bold. I thought it unlikely they would have done anything purposely to upset Traffic further and bring the stuck-up Alessandro literally down to earth, but one never knew. What I did know was that Alessandro's continuing health was essential to my own.

"George," I said, "put Traffic away in his box, and, Etty"—she was at my shoulder, clicking her tongue but not looking over-sorry—"is there anything we can use as a stretcher?"

"There's one in the tack room," she said, nodding, and told Ginge to go and get it.

The stretcher turned out to be a minimal affair of a piece of grubby green canvas slung between two uneven-shaped poles, which looked as though they might once have been a pair of oars. By the time Ginge returned with it, my heartbeat had descended from Everest: Alessandro was alive and not in too deep a coma, and Enso's pistol would not yet be popping me off in revenge to kingdom come.

As far as I could tell, none of his bones were broken, but I took exaggerated care over lifting him onto the stretcher. Etty disapproved; she would have had George and Ginge lift him up by his wrists and ankles and sling him on like a sack of corn. I, more moderately, told George and Ginge to lift him gently, carry him down to the house, and put him on the sofa in the owners' room. Following, I detoured off into the office and asked Margaret to telephone for a doctor.

Alessandro was stirring when I went into the owners' room. George and Ginge stood looking down at him, one elderly and resigned, one young and pugnacious, neither of them feeling any sympathy with the patient.

"O.K.," I said to them. "That's the lot. The doctor's coming for him."

Both of them looked as if they would like to say something, but they left without speaking and aired their opinions in the yard.

Alessandro opened his eyes, and for the first time looked a little vulnerable. He didn't know what had happened, didn't know where he was or how he had got there. The puzzlement formed new lines on his face, made it look younger and softer. Then his eyes focused on my face, and in one bound a lot of memory came back. The dove dissolved into the hawk. It was like watching the awakening of a spastic, from loose-limbed peace up to tightness and jangle.

"What happened?" he asked.

"Traffic threw you."

"Oh," he said more weakly than he liked. He shut his eyes and through his teeth emitted one heartfelt word. "Sod."

There was a sudden commotion at the door and the chauffeur plunged into the room with Margaret trying to cling to one arm. He threw her effortlessly out of his way and shaped up to do the same to me.

"What has happened?" he demanded threateningly. "What are you doing to the son?" His voice sent a shiver up my spine. If he wasn't one of the rubber faces, he sounded exactly like it.

Alessandro spoke from the sofa with tiredness in his voice; and he spoke in Italian, which, thanks to a one-time girl friend, I more or less understood.

"Stop, Carlo. Go back to the car. Wait for me. The horse threw me. Neil Griffon will not harm me. Go back to the car, and wait for me."

Carlo moved his head to and fro like a baffled bull, but finally subsided and did as he was told. Three *sotto-voce* cheers for the discipline of the Rivera household.

"A doctor is coming to see you," I said.

"I do not want a doctor."

"You're not leaving that sofa until I'm certain there is nothing wrong with you."

He sneered. "Afraid of my father?"

"Think what you like," I said; and he obviously did.

The doctor, when he came, turned out to be the same one who had once diagnosed my mumps, measles, and chicken pox. Old now, with overactive lachrymal glands and hesitant speech, he did not in the least appeal to his present patient. Alessandro treated him rudely, and got back courtesy where he deserved a smart kick.

"Nothing much wrong with the lad" was the verdict. "But he'd better stay in bed today, and rest tomorrow. That'll put you right, young man, eh?"

The young man glared back ungratefully and didn't answer. The old doctor turned to me, gave me a tolerant smile, and said to let him know if the lad had any after-effects, like dizziness or headaches.

"Old fool," said the lad audibly as I showed the doctor out; and when I went back Alessandro was already on his feet.

"Can I go now?" he asked sarcastically.

"As far and for as long as you like," I agreed.

His eyes narrowed. "You are not getting rid of me."

"Pity," I said.

After a short furious silence, he walked a little unsteadily past me and out the door. I went into the office and with Margaret watched through the window while the chauffeur bustled around, settling him comfortably into the back seat of the Mercedes; and presently, without looking back, he drove "the son" away.

"Is he all right?" Margaret asked.

"Shaken, not stirred," I said flippantly, and she laughed. But she followed the car with her eyes until it turned left down Bury Road.

He stayed away the following day but came back on the Thursday morning in time for the first lot. I was up in the top part of the yard talking to Etty when the car arrived. Her pleasant expression changed to the one of tight-lipped dislike which she always wore when Alessandro was near her, and when she saw him erupting athletically from the back seat and striding purposefully toward us, she discovered something that urgently needed seeing to in one of the bays farther down.

Alessandro noted her flight with a twist of scorn on his lips, and widened it into an irritating smirk as a greeting to me. He held out a small flat tin box, identical with the one he had presented before.

"Message for you," he said. All the cockiness was back *fortissimo,* and I would have known even without the tin that he had again been to see his father. He had recharged his malice like a battery plugged into the mains.

"Do you know what is in it, this time?"

He hesitated. "No," he said. And I believed him, because his ignorance seemed to annoy him. The tin was fastened round the edge with adhesive tape. Alessandro, with the superior smirk still in place, watched me pull it off. I rolled the tape into a small sticky ball and put it in my pocket; then carefully I opened the tin.

There was another little wooden horse between two thin layers of cotton wool.

It had a label round its neck.

It had a broken leg.

I didn't know what exactly was in my face when I looked up at Alessandro, but the smirk deteriorated into a half-anxious bravado.

"He said you wouldn't like it," he remarked defiantly.

"Come with me, then," I said abruptly. "And see if you do." I set off up the yard toward the drive, but he didn't follow; and before I reached my destination I was met by George hurrying toward me with a distressed face and worried eyes.

"Mr. Neil, Indigo's got cast and broken a leg in his box—same as Moonrock. You wouldn't think it could happen, not to two old'uns like them, not ten days apart."

"No, you wouldn't," I said grimly, and walked back with him into Indigo's box, stuffing the vicious message in its tin into my jacket pocket.

The nice-natured gelding was lying in the straw trying feebly to stand up. He kept lifting his head and pushing at the floor with one of his forefeet, but all strength seemed to have left him. The other forefoot lay uselessly bent at an unnatural angle, snapped through just above the pastern.

I squatted down beside the poor old horse and patted his neck. He lifted his head again and thrashed to get back onto his feet, then flopped limply back into the straw. His eyes looked glazed, and he was dribbling.

"Nothing to be done, George," I said. "I'll go and telephone the vet." I put only regret into my voice and kept my boiling fury to myself. George nodded resignedly but without much emotion; like every older stableman, he had seen a lot of horses die.

The young chubby Dainsee got out of his bath to answer the telephone.

"Not another one!" he exclaimed when I told him.

"I'm afraid so. And would you bring with you any gear you need for doing a blood test?"

"Whatever for?"

"I'll tell you when you get here."

"Oh." He sounded surprised, but willing to go along. "All right, then. Half a jiffy while I swap the bath towel for my natty suiting."

He came in jeans and his dirty Land-Rover twenty minutes later. Bounced out onto the gravel, nodded cheerfully, and turned at once toward Indigo's box. George was along there with the horse, but the rest of the yard stood quiet and empty. Etty, showing distress at the imminent loss of her lead horse, had taken the string down to Southfields on the racecourse side, and Alessandro presumably had gone with her, as he was nowhere about, and his chauffeur was waiting as usual in the car.

Indigo was up on his feet. George, holding him by the head-collar, said that the old boy just suddenly seemed to get his strength back and stood up, and he'd been eating some hay since then, and it was a right shame he'd got cast, that it was. I nodded and took the head-collar from him, and told him I'd see to Indigo, and he could go and get on with putting the oats through the crushing machine ready for the morning feeds.

"He makes a good yard man," Dainsee said. "Old George, he was deputy head gardener once at the Viceroy's palace in India. It accounts for all those tidy flower beds and tubs of pretty shrubs which charm the owners when they visit the yard."

I was surprised. "I didn't know that."

"Odd world." He soothed Indigo with a touch, and peered closely at the broken leg. "What's all this about a blood test?" he asked, straightening up and eying me with speculation.

"Do vets have a keep-mum tradition?"

His gaze sharpened into active curiosity. "Professional secrets, like doctors and lawyers? Yes, sure we do. As long as it's not a matter of keeping quiet about a spot of foot-and-mouth."

"Nothing like that." I hesitated. "I'd like you to run a private blood test. Could that be done?"

"How private? It'll have to go to the Equine Research Labs. I can't do it myself, haven't got the equipment."

"Just a blood sample, with no horse's name attached."

"Oh, sure. That happens all the time. But you can't really think anyone *doped* the poor old horse!"

"I think he was given an anesthetic," I said. "And that his leg was broken on purpose."

"Oh, glory." His mouth was rounded into an O of astonishment, but the eyes flickered with the rapidity of his thoughts. "You seem sane enough," he said finally, "so let's have a look-see."

He squatted down beside the affected limb and ran his fingers very lightly down over the skin. Indigo shifted under his touch and ducked and raised his head violently.

"All right, old fellow," Dainsee said, standing up again and patting his neck. He raised his eyebrows at me. "Can't say you're wrong, can't say you're right." He paused, thinking it over. The eyebrows rose and fell several times, like punctuations. "Tell you what," he said, at length. "I've got a portable X-ray machine back home. I'll bring it along, and we'll take a picture. How's that?"

"Very good idea," I said, pleased.

"Right." He opened his case, which he had parked just inside the door. "Then I'll just freeze that leg, so he'll be in no discomfort until I come back." He brought out a hypodermic and held it up against the light, beginning to press the plunger.

"Do the blood test first," I said.

"Eh?" He blinked at me. "Oh, yes, of course. Golly, yes, of course. Silly of me." He laughed gently, laid down the first syringe, and put together a much larger one, empty.

He took the sample from the jugular vein, which he found and pierced efficiently first time of asking. "Bit of luck," he murmured in self-deprecation, and drew half a tumblerful of blood into the syringe. "Have to give the lab people enough to work on, you know," he said, seeing my surprise. "You can't get reliable results from a thimbleful."

"I suppose not."

He packed the sample into his case, shot the freezing local into Indigo's near fore, nodded and blinked with undiminished cheerfulness, and smartly departed. Indigo, totally unconcerned, went back contentedly to his haynet, and I with bottled anger went into the house.

The label on the little wooden horse had "INDIGO" printed in capitals on one side of it, and on the other, also in capitals, a short sharp message: "TO HURT MY SON IS TO INVITE DESTRUCTION."

Neither George nor Etty saw any sense in the vet going away without putting Indigo down.

"Er . . . ," I said. "He found he didn't have the humane killer with him, after all. He thought it was in his bag, but it wasn't."

"Oh," they said, satisfied, and Etty told me that everything had gone well on the gallops and that Lucky Lindsay had worked a fast five furlongs and afterward wouldn't have blown out a candle.

"I put that bloody little Alex on Clip Clop and told him to take him along steadily, and he damn well disobeyed me. He shook him into a full gallop and left Lancat standing, and the touts' binoculars were working overtime."

"Stupid little fool," I said. "I'll speak to him."

"He takes every opportunity he can to cross me," she complained. "When you aren't there, he's absolutely insufferable." She took a deep, troubled breath, considering. "In fact, I think you should tell Mr. Griffon that we can't keep him."

"Next time I go to the hospital, I'll see what he says," I said. "What are you giving him to ride second lot?"

"Pulitzer," she replied promptly. "It doesn't matter so much if he doesn't do as he's told on that one."

"When you get back, tell him I want to see him before he leaves."

"Aren't you coming?"

I shook my head. "I'll stay and see to Indigo."

"I rather wanted your opinion of Pease Pudding. If he's to run in the Lincoln, we ought to give him a trial this week or next. The race is only three weeks on Saturday, don't forget."

"We could give him a half-speed gallop tomorrow and see if he's ready for a full trial," I suggested, and she grudgingly agreed that one more day would do no harm.

I watched the trim jodhpured figure walk off toward her cottage for breakfast, and would have felt flattered that she wanted my opinion had I not known why. Under an umbrella, she worked marvelously; out in the open, she felt rudderless. Even though in her heart she knew she knew more than I did, her shelter instinct had cast me as decision maker. What I needed now was a crash course in how to tell when a horse was fit. And that old joke about a crash course for pilots edged itself into a corner of my mind, like a thin gleam in the gloom.

Dainsee came back in his Land-Rover when the string had gone out for second lot, and we ran the cable for the X-ray machine through the office window and plugged it into the socket which served the mushroom heater. There seemed to be unending reinforcements of cable; it took four lengths plugged together to reach to Indigo's box, but their owner assured me that he could manage a quarter of a mile, if pushed.

He took three X-rays of the dangling leg, packed everything up again, and, almost as a passing thought, put poor old Indigo out of his troubles.

"You'll want evidence for the police," Dainsee said, shaking hands and blinking rapidly.

"No. I shan't bother the police. Not yet, anyway." He opened his mouth to protest, so I went straight on, "There are very good reasons. I can't tell you them, but they do exist."

"Oh, well, it's up to you." His eyes slid sidewise toward Moonrock's box, and his eyebrows asked the question.

"I don't know," I said. "What do you think? Looking back."

He thought for several seconds, which meant he was serious, and then said, "It would have taken a good heavy blow to smash that hock. Wouldn't have thought anyone would bother, while a pastern like Indigo's would be simple."

"Moonrock just provided the idea for Indigo?" I suggested.

"I should think so." He smiled grimly. "Mind it doesn't become an epidemic."

"I'll mind," I said thinly; and knew I would have to.

Alessandro showed no sign that Etty had given him my message about wanting to see him. He strode straight out of the yard toward his waiting car, and it was only because I happened to be looking out the office window that I caught him.

I opened the window and called to him. "Alessandro, come here a minute."

He forged straight on as if he hadn't heard, so I added, "To talk about your first races."

He stopped in one stride with a foot left in the air in indecision, then changed direction and came slowly toward the window.

"Go round into the owners' room," I said. "Where you were lying on the sofa." I shut the window, gave Margaret a whimsically rueful placating smile, which could mean whatever she thought it did, and removed myself from earshot.

Alessandro came unwillingly into the owners' room, knowing that he had been hooked. I played fair, however.

"You can have a ride in an apprentice race at Catterick in four weeks. On Pulitzer. And on condition that you don't go bragging about it in the yard and antagonizing all the other boys."

"I want to ride Archangel," he said flatly.

"It sometimes seems to me that you are remarkably intelligent and, with a great deal of application, might become a passable jockey," I said and, before his self-satisfaction smothered him, added, "and sometimes, like today, you behave so stupidly, and with such little understanding of what it takes to be what you want to be, that your ambitions look pathetic."

The thin body stiffened rigidly and the black eyes glared. Since I undoubtedly had his full attention, I made the most of it.

"These horses are here to win races. They won't win races if their training program is hashed up. If you are told to do a half-speed gallop on Clip Clop and you work him flat out and tire him beyond his capacity, you are helping to make sure he takes longer to prepare. You won't win races unless the stable does, so it is in your own interest to help train the horses to the best of your ability. Disobeying riding orders is therefore just plain stupid. Do you follow?"

The black eyes looked blacker and sank into the sockets. He didn't answer.

"Then there is this fixation of yours about Archangel. I'll let you ride him on the Heath as soon as you show you are good enough, and in particular responsible enough, to look after him. Whether you ever ride him in a race is up to you more than me. But I'm doing you a favor in starting you off on less well-known horses at smaller meetings. You may think you are brilliant, but you have only ridden against amateurs. I am giving you a chance to prove what you can do against professionals in private, and lessening the risk of you falling flat on your face at Newbury or Kempton."

The eyes were unwavering. He still said nothing.

"And Indigo," I went on, taking a grip on my anger and turning it out cold and biting, "Indigo may have been of no use to you because he no longer raced, but if you cause the death of any more of the horses, there will be just one less for you to win on."

He moved his jaw as if with an effort.

"I didn't—cause the death of Indigo."

I took the tin out of my pocket and gave it to him. He opened it slowly, compressed his mouth at the contents, and read the label.

"I didn't want ... I didn't mean him to kill Indigo." The supercilious smile had all gone. He was still hostile, but defensive. "He was angry because Traffic had thrown me."

"Did you mean him to kill Traffic, then?"

"No, I did not," he said vehemently. "As you said, what would be the point of killing a horse I could win a race on?"

"But to kill harmless old Indigo because you bumped

your head off a horse you yourself insisted on riding," I said with bitter sarcasm.

His gaze, for the first time, switched to the carpet. He was not too proud of himself.

"You didn't tell him," I guessed. "You didn't tell him that you insisted on riding Traffic."

"Miss Craig told me to," he said sullenly.

"Not the time he threw you."

He looked up again, and I would have sworn he was unhappy. "I didn't tell my father I was knocked out."

"Who did?"

"Carlo. The chauffeur."

"You could have explained that I did not try to harm you."

The unhappiness turned to a shade of desperation.

"You have met my father," he said. "It isn't always possible to tell him things, especially when he is angry. He will give me anything I ask for, but I cannot talk to him."

He went away and left me speechless.

He couldn't talk to his father.

Enso would give Alessandro anything he wanted, would smash a path for him at considerable trouble to himself, and would persist as long as Alessandro hungered, but they couldn't talk.

And I . . . I could lie and scheme and walk a tightrope to save my father's stables for him.

But talk with him, no, I couldn't.

chapter 8

"DID YOU know," Margaret said, looking up casually from her typewriter, "that Alessandro is living down the road at the Forbury Inn?"

"No, I didn't," I said. "But it doesn't surprise me. It goes with a chauffeur-driven Mercedes, after all."

"He has a double room to himself with a private bathroom, and doesn't eat enough to keep a bird alive."

"How do you know all this?"

"Susie brought a friend home from school for tea yesterday, and she turned out to be the daughter of the resident receptionist at the Forbury Inn."

"Any more fascinating intimate details?" I asked.

She smiled. "Alessandro puts on a track suit every afternoon and goes off in a car, and when he comes back he is all sweaty and has a very hot bath with nice smelly oil in it."

"The receptionist's daughter is how old?"

"Seven."

"Proper little snooper."

"All children are observant. . . . And she also said that he never talks to anyone if he can avoid it except to his chauffeur in a funny language—"

"Italian," I murmured.

". . . and that nobody likes him very much because he is pretty rude, but they like the chauffeur still less because he is even ruder."

I pondered. "Do you think," I said, "that via your daughter, via her school chum, via her receptionist parent, we could find out if Alessandro gave any sort of home address when he registered?"

"Why don't you just ask him?" she said reasonably.

"Ah," I said. "But our Alessandro is sometimes a mite contrary. Didn't you ask him when you completed his indentures?"

"He said they were moving, and had no address."

"Mm." I nodded.

"How extraordinary. . . . I can't see why he won't tell you. Well, yes, I'll ask Susie's chum if she knows."

"Great," I said, and pinned little hope on it.

Gillie wanted to come and stay at Rowley Lodge.

"How about the homeless orphans?" I said.

"I could take some weeks off. I always can. You know that. And now that you've stopped wandering round industrial towns living in one hotel after another, we could spend a bit more time together."

I kissed her nose. Ordinarily I would have welcomed her proposal. I looked at her with affection.

"No," I said. "Not just now."

"When, then?"

"In the summer."

She made a face at me, her eyes full of intelligence. "You never like to be cluttered when you are deeply involved in something."

"You're not clutter." I smiled.

"I'm afraid so. That's why you've never married. Not like most bachelors because they want to be free to sleep with any offered girl, but because you don't like your mind to be distracted."

"I'm here," I pointed out, kissing her again.

"For one night in seven. And only then because you had to come most of the way to see your father."

"My father gets visited because he's on the way to you."

"Liar," she said agreeably. "The best you can say is that it's two cats with one stone."

"Birds."

"Well, birds, then."

"Let's go eat," I said; opened the front door and closed it behind us, and packed her into the Jensen.

"Did you know that Aristotle Onassis had earned himself a whole million by the time he was twenty-eight?"

"No, I didn't know," I said.

"He beat you," she said. "By four times as much."

"He's four times the man."

Her eyes slid sidewise toward me and a smile hovered in the air. "He may be."

We stopped for a red light and then turned left beside a church with a notice board saying, "These doth the Lord hate: a proud look, a lying tongue. Proverbs 6:16–17."

"Which proverb do you think is the most stupid?" she asked.

"Um. . . . Bird in the hand is worth two in the bush."

"Why ever?"

"Because if you build a cage round the bush, you get a whole flock."

"As long as the two birds aren't both the same sex."

"You think of everything," I said admiringly.

"Oh, I try. I try."

We went up to the top of the Post Office Tower and revolved three and a half times during dinner.

"It said in the *Times* today that that paper firm you advised last autumn has gone bust," she said.

"Well. . . ." I grinned. "They didn't take my advice."

"Silly old them. What was it?"

"To sack ninety percent of the management, get some new accountants, and make peace with the unions."

"So simple, really." Her mouth twitched.

"They said they couldn't do it, of course."

"And you said?"

"Prepare to meet thy doom."

"How Biblical."

"Or words to that effect."

"Think of all those poor people thrown out of work," she said. "It can't be funny when a firm goes bust."

"The firm had hired people all along in the wrong proportions. By last autumn, they had only two productive workers for every one on the clerical, executive, and maintenance staff. Also the unions were vetoing automation, and insisting that every time a worker left another should be hired in his place."

She pensively bit into pâté and toast. "It doesn't sound as if it could have been saved at all."

"Yes, it could," I said reflectively. "But it often seems to me that people in a firm would rather see the whole ship sink than throw out half the crew and stay afloat."

"Fairer to everyone if they all drown?"

"Only the firm drowns. The people swim off and make sure they overload someone else's raft."

She licked her fingers. "You used to find sick firms fascinating."

"I still do," I said, surprised.

She shook her head. "Disillusion has been creeping in for a long time."

I looked back, considering. "It's usually quite easy to see what's wrong. But there's often a stone-wall resistance on both sides to putting it right. Always dozens of reasons why change is impossible."

"Russell Arletti rang me up yesterday," she said casually.

"Did he really?"

She nodded. "He wanted me to persuade you to leave Newmarket and do a job for him. A big one, he said."

"I can't," I said positively.

"He's taking me out to dinner on Tuesday evening to discuss, as he put it, how to wean you from the gee-gees."

"Tell him to save himself the price of a meal."

"Well, no." She wrinkled her nose. "I might just be hungry again by Tuesday. I'll go out with him. I like him. But I think I'll spend the evening preparing him for the worst."

"What worst?"

"That you won't ever be going back to work for him again."

"Gillie . . ."

"It was only a phase," she said, looking out the window at the sparkle of the million lights slowly sliding by below us. "It was just that you'd cashed in your antique chips and you weren't exactly starving, and Russell netted you on the wing, so to speak, with an interesting diversion. But you've been getting tired of it recently. You've been restless, and too full of—I don't know—too full of power. I think that after you've played with the gee-gees you'll break out in a great gust and build a new empire—much bigger than before."

"Have some wine?" I said ironically.

"And you may scoff, Neil Griffon, but you've been letting your Onassis instinct go to rust."

"Not a bad thing, really."

"You could be creating jobs for thousands of people, instead of trotting round a small town in a pair of jodh-purs."

"There's six million quids' worth in that stable," I said

slowly; and felt the germ of an idea lurch, as it sometimes did, across the ganglions.

"What are you thinking about?" she demanded. "What are you thinking about at this moment?"

"The genesis of ideas."

She gave a sigh that was half a laugh. "And that's exactly why you'll never marry me, either."

"What do you mean?"

"You like the *Times* crossword more than sex."

"Not more," I said. "First."

"Do you want me to marry you?"

She kissed my shoulder under the sheet.

"Would you?"

"I thought you were fed up with marriage." I moved my mouth against her forehead. "I thought Jeremy had put it for life."

"He wasn't like you."

He wasn't like you. . . . She said it often. Any time her husband's name cropped up. He wasn't like you.

The first time she said it, three months after I met her, I asked the obvious question.

"What was he like?"

"Fair, not dark. Willowy, not compact. A bit taller: six feet two. Outwardly more fun; inwardly infinitely more boring. He didn't want a wife so much as an admiring audience . . . and I got tired of the play." She paused. "And when Jennifer died . . ."

She had not talked about her ex-husband before that, and had always shied painfully away from the thought of her daughter. She went on, in a careful emotionless quiet voice, half muffled against my skin.

"Jennifer was killed in front of me . . . by a youth in a leather jacket on a motorcycle. We were crossing the road. He came roaring round the corner doing sixty in a built-up area. He just . . . plowed into her. . . ." A long shuddering pause. "She was eight . . . and super." She swallowed. "The boy had no insurance. . . . Jeremy raved on and on about it, as if money could have compensated . . . and we didn't need money; he'd inherited almost as much as I had. . . ." Another pause. "So anyway, after that, when he found someone else and drifted off, I was glad, really. . . ."

Though passing time had done its healing, she still had dreams about Jennifer. Sometimes she cried when she woke up, because of Jennifer.

I smoothed her shining hair. "I'd make a lousy husband."

"Oh. . . ." She took a shaky breath. "I know that. Two and a half years I've known you, and you've blown in every millennium or so, to say hi."

"But stayed awhile."

"I'll grant you."

"So what do you want?" I asked. "Would you rather be married?"

She smiled contentedly. "We'll go on as we are—if you like."

"I do like." I switched off the light.

"As long as you prove it now and again," she added unnecessarily.

"I wouldn't let anyone else hang pink-and-green curtains against ocher walls in my bedroom," I said.

"My bedroom. I rent it."

"You're in arrears. By at least eighteen months."

"I'll pay up tomorrow. . . . Hey, what are you doing?"

"I'm a businessman," I murmured, "getting down to business."

When I saw my father next, he did not make it easy for me to start a new era in father-son relationships.

He told me that as I did not seem to be making much progress in engaging someone else to take over the stable, he was going to find someone himself. By telephone.

He said he had done some of the entries for the next two weeks, and that Margaret was to type them out and send them off.

He said that Pease Pudding was to be taken out of the Lincoln.

He said that I had brought him the '64 half bottles of Bollinger, and he preferred the '61.

"You are feeling better, then," I said into the first real gap of the monologue.

"What? Oh, yes, I suppose I am. Now, did you hear what I said? Pease Pudding is not to go in the Lincoln."

"Why ever not?"

He gave me an irritated look. "How do you expect him to be ready?"

"Etty is a good judge. She says he will be."

"I will not have Rowley Lodge made to look stupid by running hopelessly undertrained horses in important races."

"If Pease Pudding runs badly, people will only say that it shows how good a trainer you are yourself."

"That is not the point," he said repressively.

I opened one of the half bottles and poured the golden bubbles into his favorite Jacobean glass, which I had brought for the purpose. Champagne would not have tasted right to him from a tooth mug. He took a sip and evidently found the '64 was bearable after all, though he didn't say so.

"The point," he explained as if to a moron, "is the stud fees. If he runs badly, his future value at stud is what will be affected."

"Yes, I understand that."

"Don't be silly, how can you? You know nothing about it."

I sat down in the visitors' armchair, leaned back, crossed my legs, and put into my voice all the reasonableness and weight which I had learned to project into industrial discussions, but which I had never before had the sense to use on my father.

"Rowley Lodge is heading for some financial rocks," I said, "and the cause of it is too much prestige-hunting. You are scared of running Pease Pudding in the Lincoln because you own a half share in him, and if he runs badly it will be your own capital investment, as well as Lady Vector's, that will suffer."

He spilled some champagne on his sheet, and didn't notice it.

I went on, "I know that it is quite normal for people to own shares in the horses they train. At Rowley Lodge just now, however, you own too many part shares for safety. I imagine you collected so many because you could not bear to see rival stables acquiring what you judged to be the next crop of world-beaters, so that you probably said to your owners something like 'If Archangel goes for forty thousand at auction and that's too much for you, I'll put up twenty thousand towards it.' So you've gathered together one of the greatest strings in the country, and their potential stud value is enormous."

He gazed at me blankly, forgetting to drink.

"This is fine," I said, "as long as the horses do win as expected. And year after year, they do. You've been pursuing this policy in moderation for a very long time, and it's made you steadily richer. But now, this year, you've overextended. You've bought too many. As all the part owners only pay part training fees, the receipts are not now covering the expenses. Not by quite a long way. As a result, the cash balance at the bank is draining away like bath water, and there are still three weeks to go before the first race, let alone the resale of the successful animals for stud. This dicey situation is complicated by your broken leg, your assistant being still in a coma from which he is unlikely to recover, and your stable apparently stagnating in the hands of a son who doesn't know how to train the horses; and all that is why you are scared silly of running Pease Pudding in the Lincoln."

I stopped for reactions. There weren't any. Just shock.

"You can, on the whole, stop worrying," I said, and knew that things would never again be quite as they had been between us. Thirty-four, I thought ruefully; I had had to be thirty-four before I entered this particular arena on equal terms. "I could sell your half share before the race."

Wheels slowly began to turn again behind his eyes. He blinked. Stared at his sloping champagne and straightened the glass.

"How—how do you know all this?" There was more resentment in his voice than anxiety.

"I looked at the account books."

"No. . . . I mean, who told you?"

"No one needed to tell me. My job for the last six years has involved reading account books and doing sums."

He recovered enough to take some judicious sips.

"At least you do understand why it is imperative we get

an experienced trainer to take over until I can get about again."

"There's no need for one," I said incautiously. "I've been there for three weeks now—"

"And do you suppose that you can learn how to train race horses in three weeks?" he asked with reviving contempt.

"Since you ask," I said, "yes." And before he turned purple, tacked on, "I was born to it, if you remember. I grew up there. I find, much to my own surprise, that it is second nature."

He saw this statement more as a threat than as a reassurance. "You're not staying on after I get back."

"No." I smiled. "Nothing like that."

He grunted. Hesitated. Gave in. He didn't say in so many words that I could carry on, but just ignored the whole subject from that point.

"I don't want to sell my half of Pease Pudding."

"Draw up a list of those you don't mind selling, then," I said. "About ten of them, for a start."

"And just who do you think is going to buy them? New owners don't grow on trees, you know. And half shares are harder to sell. Owners like to see their names in the race cards and in the press."

"I know a lot of businessmen," I said, "who would be glad to have a race horse but who actively shun the publicity. You pick out ten horses, and I'll sell your half shares."

He didn't say he would, but he picked them out, then and there. I ran my eye down the finished list and saw only one to disagree with.

"Don't sell Lancat," I said.

He bristled. "I know what I'm doing."

"He's going to be good as a three-year-old," I said. "I see from the form book that he was no great shakes at two, and if you see now you'll not get back what you paid. He's looking very well, and I think he'll win quite a lot."

"Rubbish. You don't know what you're talking about."

"All right. . . . How much would you accept for your half?"

He pursed his lips, thinking about it. "Four thousand.

You should be able to get four, with his breeding. He cost twelve, altogether, as a yearling."

"You'd better suggest prices for all of them," I said. "If you wouldn't mind."

He didn't mind. I folded the list, put it in my pocket, picked up the entry forms he had written on, and prepared to go. He held out to me the champagne glass, empty.

"Have some of this. . . . I can't manage it all."

I took the glass, refilled it, and drank a mouthful. The bubbles popped round my teeth. He watched. His expression was as severe as ever, but he nodded, sharply, twice. Not as symbolic a gesture as a pipe of peace, but just as much of an acknowledgment, in its way.

On Monday morning, tapping away, Margaret said, "Susie's friend's mum says she has just happened to see Alessandro's passport."

"Which just happened," I said dryly, "to be well hidden away in Alessandro's bedroom."

"Let us not stare at gift horses."

"Let us not," I agreed.

"Susie's friend's mum says that the address on the passport was not in Italy, but in Switzerland. A place called Bastagnola. Is that any use?"

"I hope Susie's friend's mum won't lose her job."

"I doubt it," Margaret said. "She hops into bed with the manager when his wife goes shopping in Cambridge."

"How do you know?"

Her eyes laughed. "Susie's friend told me."

I telephoned to an importer of cameras who owed me a favor and asked him if he had any contacts in the town of Bastagnola.

"Not myself. But I could establish one, if it's important."

"I want any information anyone can dig up about a man called Enso Rivera. As much information as possible."

He wrote it down and spelled it back. "See what I can do," he said.

He rang two days later and sounded subdued.

"I'll be sending you an astronomical bill for European phone calls."

"That's all right."

"An awful lot of people didn't want to talk about your man. I met an exceptional amount of resistance."

"Is he Mafia, then?" I asked.

"No. Not Mafia. In fact, he and the Mafia are not on speaking terms. On stabbing terms, maybe, but not speaking. There seems to be some sort of truce between them." He paused.

"Go on," I said.

"Well. . . . As far as I can gather—and I wouldn't swear to it—he is a sort of receiver of stolen property. Most of it in the form of currency, but some gold and silver and precious stones from melted-down jewelry. I heard—and it was at third hand from a high-up policeman, so you can believe it or not, as you like—that Rivera accepts the stuff, sells or exchanges it, takes a large commission, and banks the rest in Swiss accounts which he opens up for his clients. They can collect their money any time they like . . . and it is believed that he has an almost world-wide connection. But all this goes on behind a supposedly legitimate business as a dealer in watches. They've never managed to bring him to court. They can never get witnesses to testify."

"You've done marvels," I said.

"There's a bit more." He cleared his throat. "He has a son, apparently, that no one cares to cross. Rivera has been known to ruin people who don't immediately do what the son wants. He only has this one child. He is reputed to have deserted his wife. . . . Well, a lot of Italian men do that."

"He is Italian, then?"

"By birth, yes. He's lived in Switzerland for about fifteen years, though. Look, I don't know if you're intending to do business with him, but I got an unmistakable warning from several people to steer clear of him. They say he's dangerous. They say if you fall foul of him you wake up dead. Either that, or—well, I know you'll laugh—but there's a sort of superstition that if he looks your way you'll break a bone."

I didn't laugh. Not a chuckle.

Almost as soon as I put the receiver down, the telephone rang again. Dainsee.

"I've got your X-ray pictures in front of me," he said. "But they're inconclusive, I'm afraid. It just looks a pretty ordinary fracture. There's a certain amount of longitudinal splitting, but then there often is with cannon bones."

"What would be the simplest way to break a bone on purpose?" I asked.

"Twist it," he said promptly. "Put it under stress. A bone under stress would snap quite easily if you gave it a bang. Ask any footballer or any skater. Stress, that's what does it."

"You can't see stress on the X-rays. . . ."

"Afraid not. Can't rule it out, though. Can't rule it in, either. Sorry."

"It can't be helped."

"But the blood test," he said. "I've had the results, and you were bang on target."

"Anesthetic?"

"Yep. Some brand of promazine. Sparine, probably."

"I'm no wiser," I said. "How would you give it to a horse?"

"Injection," Dainsee said. "Very simple intramuscular injection, nothing difficult. Just punch the needle in anywhere handy. It's often used to shoot into mania patients in mental hospitals when they're raving. Puts them out for hours."

Something about promazine rang a highly personal note.

"Does the stuff work instantly?" I asked.

"If you give it intravenously, it would. But intramuscularly, what it's equally designed for, it would take a few minutes, probably. Ten to fifteen minutes on a human; don't know for a horse."

"If you injected it into a human, could you do it through clothes?"

"Oh, sure. As I said. They use it as a standby in mental hospitals. They wouldn't get people in a manic state to sit nice and quiet and roll their sleeves up."

chapter 9

For two weeks, the status at Rowley Lodge remained approximately quo.

I heavily amended my father's entry forms and sent them in, and sold six of the half shares to various acquaintances, without offering Lancat to any of them.

Margaret took to wearing green eye shadow, and Susie's friend reported that Alessandro had made a telephone call to Switzerland and didn't wear pajamas. Also that the chauffeur always paid for everything, as Alessandro didn't have any money.

Etty grew more tense as the beginning of the season drew nearer, and lines of anxiety seldom left her forehead. I was leaving a great deal more to her judgment than my father did, and she was in consequence feeling insecure. She openly ached for his return.

The horses, all the same, were working well. We had no further mishaps except that a two-year-old filly developed severe sinus trouble, and as far as I could judge from watching the performances of the forty-five other stables using Newmarket Heath, the Rowley Lodge string was as forward as any.

Alessandro turned up day after day and silently rode what and how Etty told him to, though with a ramrod spine of protest. He said no more about not taking orders from a woman, and I imagined that even he could see that without Etty there would be fewer winners on the horizon. She herself had almost stopped complaining about him and was watching him with a more objective eye, because there was no doubt that after a month's concentrated practice he was riding better than the other apprentices.

He was also growing visibly thinner, and no longer looked well. Small-framed though he might be, the six stone seven pounds that he was aiming to shrink his body down to was punitive for five foot four.

Alessandro's fanaticism was an awkward factor. If I had imagined that by making the going as rough as I dared he would give up his idle fancy and depart, I had been wrong. This was no idle fancy. It was revealing itself all too clearly as a consuming ambition: an ambition strong enough to make him starve himself, take orders from a woman, and perform what were evidently miracles of self-discipline, considering that it was probably the first time in his life that he had had to use any.

Against Etty's wishes, I put him up one morning on Archangel.

"He's not ready for that," she protested when I told her I was going to.

"There isn't another lad in the yard who will take more care of him," I said.

"But he hasn't the experience."

"He has, you know. Archangel is only more valuable, not more difficult to ride, than the others."

Alessandro received the news not with joy but with an "at last" expression, more scorn than patience. We went down to the Waterhall Center, away from public gaze, and there Archangel did a fast six furlongs and pulled up looking as if he had just walked out of his box.

"He had him balanced," I said to Etty. "All the way."

"Yes, he did," she said grudgingly. "Pity he's such an obnoxious little squirt."

Alessandro returned with an "I told you so" face, which I wiped off by saying he would be switched to Lancat tomorrow.

"Why?" he demanded furiously. "I rode Archangel very well."

"Well enough," I agreed. "And you can ride him again, in a day or two. But I want you to ride Lancat in a trial on Wednesday, so you can go out on him tomorrow, as well, and get used to him. And after the trial I want you to tell me your opinion of the horse and how he went. And I don't want one of your short sneering comments, but a thought-out assessment. It is almost as important for a jockey to be able to analyze what a horse has done in a race as ride it. Trainers depend quite a lot on what their jockeys can tell them. So you can tell me about Lancat, and I'll listen."

He gave me a long concentrating stare, but for once without the habitual superciliousness.

"All right," he said. "I will."

We held the trial on the Wednesday afternoon on the

trial ground past the Limekilns, a long way out of
Newmarket. Much to Etty's disgust, I had timed the trial
to start at exactly the same moment as the Champion
Hurdle started at Cheltenham, and she wanted to watch it
on television. But the stratagem worked. We achieved the
well-nigh impossible, a full-scale trial without an observer
or a tout in sight.

Apart from the two Etty and I rode, we took only four
horses along; Pease Pudding, Lancat, Archangel, and one
of the previous year's most prolific winners, a four-year-
old colt called Subito, whose best distance was a mile.
Tommy Hoylake drove up from his home in Berkshire to
ride Pease Pudding, and we put Andy on Archangel and a
taciturn lad called Faddy on the chestnut Subito.

"Don't murder them," I said before they started. "If
you feel them falter, just ease off."

Four nods. Four fidgeting colts, glossy and eager.

Etty and I hacked round to within a hundred yards of
where the trial ground ended, and when we had pulled up
in a useful position for watching, she waved a large white
handkerchief above her head. The horses started toward
us, moving fast and still accelerating, with the riders
crouched forward on their withers, heads down, reins very
short, feet against the horses' moving shoulders.

They passed still going all out, and pulled up a little
farther on. Archangel and Pease Pudding ran the whole
gallop stride for stride, and finished together. Lancat,
from starting level, lost ten lengths, made up eight, lost
two again, but still moved easily. Subito was ahead of
Lancat at the beginning, behind him when he moved up
quickly, and alongside when they passed Etty and me.

She turned to me with a deeply worried expression.

"Pease Pudding can't be ready for the Lincoln if Lancat can finish so near him. In fact, the way Lancat finished means that neither Archangel nor Subito are as far
on as I thought."

"Calm down, Etty," I said. "Relax. Take it easy. Just
turn it the other way round."

She frowned. "I don't understand you. Mr. Griffon will
be very worried when he hears—"

"Etty," I interrupted. "Did Pease Pudding, or did he
not, seem to you to be moving fast and easily?"

"Well, yes, I suppose so," she said doubtfully.

"Then it may be Lancat who is much better than you expected, not the others who are worse."

She looked at me, her face screwed up with indecision. "But Alex is only an apprentice, and Lancat was useless last year."

"In what way was he useless?"

"Oh . . . sprawly. Babyish. Had no action."

"Nothing sprawly about him today," I pointed out.

"No," she admitted slowly. "You're right. There wasn't."

The riders walked toward us, leading the horses, and Etty and I dismounted to hear what they had to say. Tommy Hoylake, built like a twelve-year-old boy with a forty-three-year-old man's face sitting incongruously on top, said, in his comfortable Berkshire accent, that he had thought that Pease Pudding had run an excellent trial until he saw Lancat pulling up so close behind him. He had ridden Lancat a good deal the previous year, and hadn't thought much of him.

Andy said Archangel went beautifully, considering the Guineas was nearly six weeks away, and Faddy, in his high-pitched finicky voice, said Subito had only been a pound or two behind Pease Pudding last year, in his opinion, and he could have been nearer to him if he had really tried. Tommy and Andy shook their heads. If they had really tried, they, too, could have gone faster.

"Alessandro?" I said.

He hesitated. "I—I lost ground at the beginning because I didn't realize— I didn't expect them to go so fast. When I asked him, Lancat just shot forward—and I could have kept him nearer to Archangel at the end, only he did seem to tire a bit, and you said—" He stopped, his voice, so to speak, on one foot.

"Good," I said. "You did right." I hadn't expected him to be so honest. For the first time since his arrival, he had made an objective self-assessment, but my faint and even slightly patronizing praise was enough to bring back the smirk. Etty looked at him with uncontrolled dislike, which didn't disturb Alessandro one little bit.

"I hardly need to remind you," I said to all of them, ignoring the displayed emotions, "to keep this afternoon's

doings to yourselves. Tommy, you can count on Pease
Pudding in the Lincoln and Archangel in the Guineas,
and if you'll come back to the office now we'll go through
your other probable rides for the next few weeks."

Alessandro's smirk turned sour, and the look he cast on
Tommy was pure Rivera. Actively dangerous: inured to
murder. Any appearance he might have given of being
even slightly tamed was suddenly as reliable as sunlight on
quicksand. I remembered the unequivocal message of
Enso's gun pointing at my chest: that if killing seemed de-
sirable, killing would quite casually be done. I had put
Tommy Hoylake in jeopardy, and I'd have to get him out.

I sent the others on ahead and told Alessandro to stay
for a minute. When the others were too far away to hear,
I said, "You will have to accept that Tommy Hoylake will
be riding as first jockey to the stable."

I got the full stare treatment, black, wide, and ill-inten-
tioned. I could almost feel the hate which flowed out of
him like hot waves across the cool March air.

"If Tommy Hoylake breaks his leg," I said clearly, "I'll
break yours."

It shook him, though he tried not to show it.

"Also, it would be pointless to put Tommy Hoylake out
of action, as I would then engage someone else. Not you.
Is that clear?"

He didn't answer.

"If you want to be a top jockey, you've got to do it
yourself. You've got to be good enough. You've got to
fight your own battles. It's no good thinking your father
will destroy everyone who stands in your way. If you are
good enough, no one will stand in your way; and if you
are not, no amount of ruining others will make you."

Still no sound. But fury, yes. Signifying all too much.

I said seriously, "If Tommy Hoylake comes to any
harm whatsoever, I will see that you never ride in another
race. At whatever consequence to myself."

He removed the stare from my face and scattered it
over the wide windy spread of the Heath.

"I am accustomed—" he began arrogantly, and then
stopped.

"I know what you are accustomed to," I said. "To having your own way at any expense to others. Your own

way, bought in misery, pain, and fear. Well, you should have settled for something that could be paid for. No amount of death and destruction will buy you ability."

"All I wanted was to ride Archangel in the Derby," he said defensively.

"Just like that? Just a whim?"

He turned his head toward Lancat and gathered together the reins. "It started like that," he said indistinctly, and walked away from me in the direction of Newmarket.

He came and rode out as usual the following morning, and the days after. News that the trial had taken place got around, and I heard that I had chosen the time of the Champion Hurdle so that I could keep the unfit state of Pease Pudding decently concealed. The antepost price lengthened, and I put a hundred pounds on him at twenty-to-one.

My father shook the *Sporting Life* at me in a rage and insisted that the horse should be withdrawn.

"Have a bit on him instead," I said. "I have."

"You don't know what you're doing."

"Yes, I do."

"It says here. . . ." He was practically stuttering with the frustration of not being able to get out of bed and thwart me. "It says here that if the trial was unsatisfactory, nothing more could be expected, with me away."

"I read it," I said. "That's just a guess. And it wasn't unsatisfactory, if you want to know. It was very encouraging."

"You're crazy," he said loudly. "You're ruining the stable. I won't have it. I won't have it, do you hear?"

"Do calm down," I said reasonably. "You'll give yourself a heart attack."

He glared at me. A hot amber glare, not a cold black one. It made a change.

"I'll send Tommy Hoylake to see you," I said. "You can ask him what he thinks."

Three days before the racing season started, I walked into the office at two-thirty to see if Margaret wanted me to sign any letters before she left to collect her children,

and found Alessandro with her, sitting on the edge of her
desk. He was wearing a navy-blue track suit and heavy
white running shoes, and his black hair was damp with
sweat and had crisped into curls.

She was looking up at him with obvious arousal, her
face slightly flushed as if someone had given all her senses
a friction rub.

She caught sight of me before he did, as he had his
back to the door. She looked away from him in confusion,
and he turned to see who had disturbed them.

There was a smile on the thin sallow face. A real smile,
warm and uncomplicated, wrinkling the skin round the
eyes and lifting the upper lip to show good teeth. For two
seconds, I saw an Alessandro I wouldn't have guessed ex-
isted, and then the light went out inside and the facial
muscles gradually reshaped themselves into the familiar
lines of wariness and annoyance.

He slid his slight weight to the floor and wiped away
with a thumb some of the sweat that stood out on his
forehead and trickled down in front of his ears.

"I want to know what horses I am going to ride this
week at Doncaster," he said. "Now that the season is
starting, you can give me horses to race."

Margaret looked at him in astonishment, for he had
sounded very much the boss. I answered him in a manner
and tone carefully lacking in both apology and aggression.

"We have only one entry at Doncaster, which is Pease
Pudding in the Lincoln on Saturday, and Tommy
Hoylake rides it," I said. "And the reason we have only
one entry"—I went straight on, as I saw the anger strok-
ing up at what he believed to be a blocking movement on
my part—"is that my father was involved in a motor accident the week these entries should have been made, and
they were never sent in."

"Oh," he said blankly.

"Still," I said, "it would be a good idea for you to go to
the races every day, to see what goes on, so that you don't
make any crashing mistakes next week."

I didn't add that I intended to do the same myself. It
never did to show all your weaknesses to the opposition.

"You can start on Pulitzer on Wednesday at Catterick,"
I said. "And after that, it's up to you."

There was a flash of menace in the black eyes.

"No," he said, a bite in his voice. "It's up to my father."

He turned abruptly on one toe and, without looking back, trotted out of the office into the yard, swerved left, and set off at a steady jog up the drive toward Bury Road. We watched him through the window, Margaret with a smile tinged with puzzlement and I with more apprehension than I liked.

"He ran all the way to the Boy's Grave and back," she said. "He says he weighed six stone twelve before he set off today, and he's lost twenty-two pounds since he came here. That sounds an awful lot, doesn't it? Twenty-two pounds, for someone as small as him."

"Severe," I said, nodding.

"He's strong, though. Like wire."

"You like him," I said, making it hover on the edge of a question.

She gave me a quick glance. "He's interesting."

I slouched into the swivel chair and read through the letters she pushed across to me. All of them in economic, good English, perfectly typed.

"If we win the Lincoln," I said, "you can have a raise."

"Thanks very much." A touch of irony. "I hear the *Sporting Life* doesn't think much of my chances."

I signed three of the letters and started reading the fourth. "Does Alessandro often call in?" I asked casually.

"First time he's done it."

"What did he want?" I asked.

"I don't think he wanted anything, particularly. He said he was going past, and just came in."

"What did you talk about?"

She looked surprised at the question but answered without comment.

"I asked him if he liked the Forbury Inn and he said he did, that it was much more comfortable than a house his father had rented on the outskirts of Cambridge. He said anyway his father had given up that house now and gone back home to do some business." She paused, thinking back, the memory of his company making her eyes smile, and I reflected that the house at Cambridge must have been where the rubber faces took me, and that there was now no point in speculating more about it.

"I asked him if he had always liked riding horses and he said yes, and I asked him what his ambitions were and he said to win the Derby and be Champion Jockey, and I said that there wasn't an apprentice born who didn't want that."

I turned my head to glance at her. "He said he wanted to be Champion Jockey?"

"That's right."

I stared gloomily down at my shoes. The skirmish had been a battle, the battle was in danger of becoming war, and now it looked as if hostilities could crackle on for months. Escalation seemed to be setting in in a big way.

"Did he ask *you* anything?"

"No. At least . . . Yes, I suppose he did." She seemed surprised, thinking about it.

"What?"

"He asked if you or your father owned any of the horses. . . . I told him your father had half shares in some of them, and he said did he own any of them outright. I said Buckram was the only one . . . and he said"—she frowned, concentrating— "he said he supposed it would be insured like the others, and I said it wasn't, actually, because Mr. Griffon had cut back on his premiums this year, so he'd better be extra careful with it on the roads." She suddenly sounded anxious. "There wasn't any harm in telling him, was there? I mean, I didn't think there was anything secret about Mr. Griffon owning Buckram."

"There isn't," I said comfortingly. "It runs in his name, for a start. It's public knowledge that he owns it."

She looked relieved and the lingering smile crept back round her eyes, and I didn't tell her that it was the bit about insurance that I found disturbing.

One of the firms I had advised in their troubles was assemblers of electronic equipment. Since they had, in fact, reorganized themselves from top to bottom and were now delighting their shareholders, I rang up the chief executive and asked for help for myself.

Urgently, I said. In fact, today. And it was half past three already.

A sharp "Phew" followed by some tongue-clicking, and the offer came. If I would drive toward Coventry, their Mr. Wallis would meet me at Kettering. He would bring what I wanted with him, and explain how I was to install it, and would that do?

It would do very well indeed, I said; and did the chief executive happen to be in need of half a race horse?

He laughed. On the salary cut I had persuaded him to take? I must be joking, he said.

Our Mr. Wallis, all of nineteen, met me in a businesslike truck and blinded me with science. He repeated the instructions clearly and twice, and then obviously doubted whether I could carry them out. To him the vagaries of the photoelectric effect were home ground, but he also realized that to the average fool they were not. He went over it again to make sure I understood.

"What is your position with the firm?" I asked at the end.

"Deputy Sales Manager," he said happily. "And they tell me I have you to thank."

I quite easily, after the lecture, installed the early-warning system at Rowley Lodge: basically a photoelectric cell linked to an alarm buzzer. After dark, when everything was quiet, I hid the necessary ultraviolet-light source in the flowering plant in a tub which stood against the end wall of the four outside boxes, and the cell itself I camouflaged in a rosebush outside the office window. The cable from this led through the office window, across the lobby, and into the owners' room, with a switch box handy to the sofa.

Soon after I had finished rigging it, Etty walked into the yard from her cottage for her usual last look round before going to bed, and the buzzer rasped out loud and clear. Too loud, I thought. A silent intruder might just hear it. I put a cushion over it, and the muffled buzz sounded like a bumblebee caught in a drawer.

I switched the noise off. When Etty left the yard, it started again immediately. Hurrah for the Deputy Sales Manager, I thought, and slept in the owners' room with my head on the cushion.

No one came.

Stiffly, at six o'clock, I got up and rolled up the cable, and collected and stowed all the gear in a cupboard in the owners' room; and when the first of the lads ambled yawning into the yard, I headed directly to the coffeepot.

Tuesday night, no one came.

Wednesday, Margaret mentioned that Susie's friend had reported two Swiss phone calls, one outgoing by Alessandro, one incoming to the chauffeur.

Etty, more anxious than ever, with the Lincoln only three days away, was snapping at the lads, and Alessandro stayed behind after second exercise and asked me if I had reconsidered and would put him up on Pease Pudding in place of Tommy Hoylake.

We were outside in the yard, with the late-morning bustle going on all around. Alessandro looked tense and hollow-eyed.

"You must know I can't," I said reasonably.

"My father says I am to tell you that you must."

I slowly shook my head. "For your own sake, you shouldn't. If you rode it, you would make a fool of yourself. Is that what your father wants?"

"He says I must insist." He was adamant.

"O.K.," I said. "You've insisted. But Tommy Hoylake is going to ride."

"But you must do what my father says," he protested.

I smiled at him faintly but didn't answer, and he did not seem to know what to say next.

"Next week, though," I said matter-of-factly, "you can ride Buckram in a race at Aintree. I entered him there especially for you. He won first time out last year, so he should have a fair chance again this time."

He just stared; didn't even blink. If there was anything to be given away, he didn't give it.

At three o'clock Thursday morning, the buzzer went off with enthusiasm three inches from my eardrum and I nearly fell off the sofa. I switched off the noise, got to my feet, and took a look into the yard through the owners' room window.

Moving quickly through the moonless night went one single small light, very faint, directed at the ground. Then, as I watched, it swung round, paused on some of the numbers of the boxes in bay four, and settled inexorably on the one which housed Buckram.

Treacherous little bastard, I thought. Finding out which horse he could kill without the owner wailing a complaint: an uninsured horse, in order to kick Rowley Lodge the harder in the financial groin.

Telling him Buckram might win him a race hadn't stopped him. Treacherous, callous little bastard.

I was out through the ready left-ajar doors and down the yard, moving silently on rubber shoes. I heard the bolts drawn quietly back and the doors squeak in their hinges, and homed on the small flicking light with far from charitable intentions.

No point in wasting time. I swept my hand down on the switch and flooded Buckram's box with a hundred watts.

I took in at a glance the syringe held, in a stunned second of suspended animation, in the gloved hand, and noticed the truncheon lying on the straw just inside the door.

It wasn't Alessandro. Too heavy. Too tall. The figure turning purposefully toward me, dressed in black from neck to foot, was one of the rubber faces.

In his rubber face.

chapter 10

THIS TIME, I didn't waste my precious advantage. I sprang straight at him and chopped with all my strength at the wrist of the hand that held the syringe.

A direct hit. The hand flew backward, the fingers opened, and the syringe spun away through the air.

I kicked his shin and punched him in the stomach, and when his head came forward I grabbed hold of it and swung him with a crash against the wall.

Buckram kicked up a fuss and stamped around loose, as rubber face had not attempted to put the head-collar on. When rubber face rushed me with jabbing fists, I caught hold of his clothes and threw him against Buckram, who snapped at him with his teeth.

A muffled sound came through the rubber, which I declined to interpret as an appeal for peace. Once away from the horse, he came at me again, shoulders hunched, head down, arms stretching forward. I stepped straight into his grasp, ignored a bash in my short ribs, put my arm tight round his neck, and banged his head on the nearest wall. The legs turned to latex to match the face, and the lids palely shut inside the eyeholes. I gave him another small crack against the wall to remove any lingering doubts, and stood back a pace. He lay feebly in the angle between floor and wall, one hand twisting slowly forward and backward across the straw.

I tied up Buckram, who by some miracle had not pushed his way out of the unbolted door and roused the neighborhood, and in stepping away from the tethering ring I nearly put my foot right down on the syringe. It lay under the manger, in the straw, and had survived undamaged through the rumpus.

I picked it up, tossed it lightly in my hand, and decided that the gifts of the gods should not be wasted. Pulling up the sleeve of rubber face's black jersey, I pushed the needle firmly into his arm and gave him the benefit of half the contents. Prudence, not compassion, stopped me from squirting in the lot; it might be that what the syringe held was a flattener for a horse but curtains for a man, and murdering was not going to help.

I pulled off rubber face's rubber face. Underneath it was Carlo. Surprise, surprise.

The prizes of war now amounted to one rubber mask, one half-empty syringe, and one bone-breaking truncheon. After a slight pause for thought, I wiped my fingerprints off the syringe, removed Carlo's gloves, and planted his fingerprints all over it; both hands. A similar liberal sprinkling went onto the truncheon; then, using the gloves to hold them with, I took the two incriminating articles up to the house and hid them temporarily in a lacquered box under a dust sheet in one of the ten unused bedrooms.

From the window on the stairs on the way down, I caught an impression of a large pale shape in the drive near the gate. Went to look, to make sure. No mistake: the Mercedes.

Back in Buckram's box, Carlo slept peacefully, totally out. I felt his pulse, which was slow but regular, and looked at my watch. Not yet three-thirty. Extraordinary.

Carrying Carlo to the car looked too much of a chore, so I went and fetched the car to Carlo. The engine started with a click and a purr, and made too little noise in the yard even to disturb the horses. Leaving the engine running, I opened both rear doors and lugged Carlo in backward. I had intended to do him the courtesy of the back seat, since he had done as much for me, but he fell limply off onto the floor. I bent his knees up, as he lay on his back, and gently shut him in.

As far as I could tell, no one saw our arrival at the Forbury Inn. I parked the Mercedes next to the other cars near the front door, switched off the engine and the side lights, and quietly went away.

By the time I had walked the near mile home, collected the rubber mask from Buckram's box and taken off his head-collar, and dismantled the electronic eye and stowed it in the cupboard, it was too late to bother with going to bed. I slept for an hour or so more on the sofa, and woke up feeling dead tired and not a bit full of energy for the first day of the races.

Alessandro arrived late, on foot, and worried.

I watched him, first through the office window and then from the owners' room, as he made his way down into the yard. He hovered in indecision in bay four, and with curiosity overcoming caution, made a crablike traverse over to Buckram's box. He unbolted the top half of the door, looked inside, and then bolted the door again. Unable from a distance to read his reaction, I walked out of the house into his sight without appearing to take any notice of him.

He removed himself smartly from bay four and pretended to be looking for Etty in bay three, but finally his uncertainty got the better of him and he turned to come and meet me.

"Do you know where Carlo is?" he asked without preamble.

"Where would you expect him to be?" I said.

He blinked. "In his room. I knock on his door when I am ready—but he wasn't there. Have you—have you seen him?"

"At four o'clock this morning," I said casually, "he was fast asleep in the back of your car. I imagine he is still there."

He turned his head away as if I'd pushed him.

"He came, then," he said, and sounded hopeless.

"He came," I agreed.

"But you didn't—I mean—kill him?"

"I'm not your father," I said. "Carlo got injected with some stuff he brought for Buckram."

His head snapped back and his eyes held a fury that was for once not totally directed at me.

"I told him not to come," he said angrily. "I told him not to."

"Because Buckram could win for you next week?"

"Yes . . . no . . . You confuse me."

"But he disregarded you and obeyed your father?"

"I told him not to come," he repeated.

"He wouldn't dare disobey your father," I said dryly.

"No one disobeys my father," he stated automatically, and then looked at me in bewilderment. "Except you," he said.

"The knack with your father," I explained, "is to dis-obey within the area where retaliation becomes progres-sively less profitable, and to widen that area at every op-portunity."

"I don't understand."

"I'll explain it to you on the way to Doncaster," I said.

"I am not coming with you," he said stiffly. "Carlo will drive me in my own car."

"He'll be in no shape to. If you want to go to the races, I think you'll find you either have to drive yourself or come with me."

He gave me an angry stare and didn't admit he couldn't drive. But he couldn't resist the attraction of the races, ei-ther, and I had counted on it.

"Very well. I will come with you."

After we had ridden back from the racecourse side with the first lot, I told him to talk to Margaret in the office while I changed into racegoing clothes, and then I drove him up to the Forbury Inn for him to do the same.

He bounded out of the Jensen almost before it stopped rolling and wrenched open one of the Mercedes' rear doors. Inside the car, a hunched figure sitting on the back seat showed that Carlo was at least partially awake, if not a hundred percent receptive to the torrent of Italian abuse breaking over him.

I tapped Alessandro on the back and, when he momen-tarily stopped cursing, said, "If he feels anything like I did after similar treatment, he will not be taking much notice. Why don't you do something constructive, like getting ready to go to the races?"

"I'll do what I please," he said fiercely, but the next minute it appeared that what pleased him was to change for the races.

While he was indoors, Carlo made one or two remarks in Italian which stretched my knowledge of the language too far. The gist, however, was clear. Something to do with my ancestors.

Alessandro reappeared wearing the dark suit he had first arrived in, which was now a full size too large. It made him look even thinner, and a good deal younger,

and almost harmless. I reminded myself sharply that a
lowered guard invited the uppercut, and jerked my head
for him to get into the Jensen.

When he had closed the door, I spoke to Carlo through
the open window of the Mercedes. "Can you hear what I
say?" I said. "Are you listening?"

He raised his head with an effort and gave me a look
which showed that he was, even if he didn't want to.

"Good," I said. "Now, take this in. Alessandro is coming with me to the races. Before I bring him back, I intend to telephone to the stables to make quite sure that no
damage of any kind has been done there—that all the
horses are alive and well. If you have any idea of going
back today to finish off what you didn't do last night, you
can drop it. Because if you do any damage you will not
get Alessandro back tonight—or for many nights—and I
cannot think that Enso Rivera would be very pleased with
you."

He looked as furious as his sorry state would let him.

"You understand?" I said.

"Yes." He closed his eyes and groaned. I left him to it
with reprehensible satisfaction.

"What did you say to Carlo?" Alessandro demanded as
I swept him away down the drive.

"Told him to spend the day in bed."

"I don't believe you."

"Words to that effect."

He looked suspiciously at the beginnings of a smile I
didn't bother to repress, and then, crossly, straight ahead
through the windscreen.

After ten silent miles, I said, "I've written a letter to
your father. I'd like you to send it to him."

"What letter?"

I took an envelope out of my inner pocket and handed
it to him.

"I want to read it," he said aggressively.

"Go ahead. It isn't stuck. I thought I would save you
the trouble."

He compressed his mouth and pulled out the letter.

He read:

Enso Rivera,

The following points are for your consideration.

1. While Alessandro stays, and wishes to stay, at Rowley Lodge, the stable must remain unharmed.

Following any form or degree of destruction, or of attempted destruction, of the stables, the Jockey Club will immediately be informed of everything that has passed, with the result that Alessandro would be banned for life from riding races anywhere in the world.

2. Tomy Hoylake.

Should any harm of any description come to Tommy Hoylake, or to any other jockey employed by the stable, the information will be laid, and Alessandro will ride no more races.

3. Moonrock, Indigo, and Buckram.

Should any further attempts be made to injure or kill any of the horses at Rowley Lodge, information will be laid, and Alessandro will ride no more races.

4. The information which would be laid consists at present of a full account of all pertinent events, together with (a) the two model horses and their handwritten labels; (b) the results of an analysis done at the Equine Research Laboratory on a blood sample taken from Indigo showing the presence of the anesthetic promazine; (c) X-ray pictures of the fracture of Indigo's near foreleg; (d) one rubber mask, worn by Carlo; and (e) one hypodermic syringe containing traces of anesthetic, and (f) one truncheon, both bearing Carlo's fingerprints.

These items are all lodged with a solicitor, who has instructions for their use in the event of my death.

Bear in mind that the case against you and your son does not have to be proved in a court of law, but only to the satisfaction of the Stewards of the Jockey Club. It is they who take away jockeys' licenses. If no further damage is done or attempted at Rowley Lodge, I will agree on my part to give Alessandro every reasonable opportunity of becoming a proficient and successful jockey.

He read the letter through twice. Then he slowly folded it and put it back in the envelope.

"He won't like it," he said. "He never lets anyone threaten him."

"He shouldn't have tried threatening me," I said mildly.

"He thought it would be your father . . . and old people frighten more easily, my father says."

I took my eyes off the road for two seconds to glance at him. He was no more disturbed by what he had just said than when he had said his father would kill me. Frightening and murdering had been the background to his childhood, and he still seemed to consider them normal.

"Do you really have all those things?" he asked. "The blood-test results . . . and the syringe?"

"I do indeed."

"But Carlo always wears gloves—" He stopped.

"He was careless," I said.

He brooded over it. "If my father makes Carlo break any more horses' legs, will you really get me warned off?"

"I certainly will."

"But after that you would have no way of stopping him from destroying the stables in revenge."

"Would he do that?" I asked. "Would he bother?"

Alessandro gave me a pitying, superior smile. "My father would be revenged if someone ate the cream cake he wanted."

"Do you approve of vengeance?" I said.

"Of course."

"It wouldn't get you back your license," I pointed out, "and anyway I doubt whether he could actually do it, because there would then be no bar to police protection and the loudest possible publicity."

He said stubbornly, "There wouldn't be any risk at all if you would agree to my riding Pease Pudding and Archangel."

"It never was possible for you to ride them without any experience, and if you'd had any sense you would have known it. So, although there's always a risk in opposing extortion, in some cases it is the only thing to do. And starting from there, it's just a matter of finding ways of opposing that don't land you in the morgue emptyhanded."

There was another long pause while we skirted Grantham and Newark. It started raining. I switched on the wipers and the blades clicked like metronomes over the glass.

"It seems to me," Alessandro said glumly, "as if you

and my father have been engaged in some sort of fight to see who is stronger, with me being the one that both of you push around."

I smiled, surprised both at his perception and that he should have said it aloud.

"That's right," I agreed. "That's how it's been from the beginning."

"Well, I don't like it."

"It only happened because of you. And if you give up the idea of being a jockey, it will all stop."

"But I *want* to be a jockey," he said, as if that were the end of it. And as far as his doting father was concerned, it was. The beginning of it, and the end of it.

Ten wet miles farther on, he said, "You tried to get rid of me, when I came."

"Yes, I did."

"Do you still want me to leave?"

"Would you?" I sounded hopeful.

"No," he said. "Because between you, you and my father have made it impossible for me to go to any other stable and start again."

A long pause. "And anyway," he said, "I don't want to go to any other stable. I want to stay at Rowley Lodge."

"And be Champion Jockey?" I murmured.

"I only told Margaret," he said sharply, and then put a couple of things together. "She told you I asked about Buckram," he said bitterly. "And that's how you caught Carlo."

In justice to Margaret, I said, "She wouldn't have told me if I hadn't directly asked her what you wanted."

"You don't trust me," he complained.

"Well, no," I said ironically. "Wouldn't I be a fool to?"

The rain fell more heavily against the windscreen. We stopped at a red light in Bawtry and waited while a lollipop man shepherded half a school across in front of us.

"That bit in your letter about helping me to be a good jockey—do you mean it?"

"Well, yes, I do," I said. "You ride well enough at home. Better than I expected, to be honest."

"I told you—" he began, lifting the arching nose.

"That you were brilliant," I finished, nodding. "So you did."

"Don't laugh at me." The ready fury boiled up.

"All you've got to do is win a few races, keep your head, show a judgment of pace and an appreciation of tactics, and stop relying on your father."

He was unpacified. "It is natural to rely on one's father," he said stiffly.

"I ran away from mine when I was sixteen."

He turned his head. I could see out of the corner of my eye that he was both surprised and unimpressed.

"Obviously he did not, like mine, give you everything you wanted."

"No," I agreed. "I wanted freedom."

I spent most of the afternoon meeting the people who knew my father: other trainers, jockeys, officials, and some of the owners. They were all without exception helpful and informative, so that by the end of the day I had learned what I would be expected (and, just as importantly, not expected) to do in connection with Pease Pudding for the Lincoln.

Tommy Hoylake, with an expansive grin, put in succinctly. "Declare it, saddle it, watch it win, and stick around in case of objections."

"Do you think we have any chance?"

"Oh, we must have," he said. "It's an open race, anything could win. Lap of the gods, you know. Lap of the gods." By which I gathered that he still hadn't made up his mind about the trial, whether Lancat was good or Pease Pudding bad.

On the drive back to Newmarket, I asked Alessandro how he had got on. As his expression whenever I had caught sight of him during the afternoon had been a mixture of envy and pride, I knew without him telling me that he had been both titillated to be recognizable as a jockey, because of his size, and enraged that a swarm of others should have started the season without him. The look he had given the boy who had won the apprentice race would have frightened a rattlesnake.

"I cannot wait until next Wednesday," he said. "I wish to begin tomorrow."

"We have no runners before next Wednesday," I said calmly.

"Pease Pudding." He was fierce. "On Saturday."

"We've been through all that."

"I wish to ride him."

"No."

He seethed away in the passenger seat. The actual sight and sound and smell of the races had excited him extraordinarily—to the pitch where he could scarcely keep still. The approach to reasonableness which had been made on the way up had all blown away in the squally wind on Doncaster's Town Moor, and the first half of the journey back was a complete waste, as far as I was concerned. Finally, though, the extreme tenseness left him, and he slumped back in his seat in some species of gloom.

I felt it would be all right then to talk to him further. I said, "What sort of a race do you think you should ride on Pulitzer?"

His spine straightened again instantly.

"I looked up his last year's form," he said. "Pulitzer was consistent; he came third or fourth or sixth, mostly. He was always near the front for most of the race but then faded out in the last furlong. Next Wednesday at Catterick, it is seven furlongs. I know that the low numbers are the best to draw, so I would hope for one of those. Then I will try to get away well at the start and take a position next to the rails, or with only one other horse inside me, and I will not go too fast, but not too slow either. I will try to stay not farther back than two and a half lengths behind the leading horse, but I will not try to get to the front until right near the end. The last sixty yards, I think. And I will try to be in front only about fifteen yards before the winning post. I think he does not race his best if he is in front, so he mustn't be in front very long."

To say I was surprised is to get nowhere near the queer excitement which rose sharply and unexpectedly in my brain. I'd had years of practice in sorting the genuine from the phony, and what Alessandro had said rang of pure sterling.

"O.K.," I said casually. "That sounds all right. You ride him just like that. And how about Buckram? You'll

be riding him in the apprentice race at Liverpool the day
after Pulitzer. Also you can ride Lancat at Teesside two
days later, on the Saturday."

"I'll look them up, and think about them," he said seriously.

"Don't bother with Lancat's form," I reminded him.
"He was no good as a two-year-old. Work from what you
learned during the trial."

"Yes," he said. "I understand."

I could see at last how to make Enso retract his threats.
But it seemed to me very likely that the future would be
more dangerous than the past.

chapter 11

EVERY EVENING during the week before the Lincoln, I spent hours answering the telephone. One owner after another rang up, and without exception sounded depressed. This, I discovered—after the fourth in a row had said, in more or less identical words, "Can't expect much with your father chained to his bed"—was because the invalid in question had been extremely busy on the blower himself.

It seems he had rung them all up, apologized for my presence, told them to expect nothing, and promised them that everything would be restored to normal as soon as he got back. He had also told his co-owner of Pease Pudding, a Major Barnette, that in his opinion the horse was not fit to run; and it had taken me half an hour of my very best persuasive tongue to convince the Major that as my father hadn't seen the horse for the past six weeks, he didn't actually know.

Looking into his activities more closely, I found that my father had also written privately every week to Etty for progress reports and had told her not to tell me she was sending them. I practically bullied this last gem out of her on the morning before the Lincoln, having cottoned on to what was happening only through mentioning that my father had told all the owners the horses were unfit. Something guilty in her expression had given her away, but she fended off my bitterness by claiming that she hadn't actually said they were unfit; that was just the way my father had chosen to interpret things.

I went into the office and asked Margaret if my father had telephoned or written to her for private reports. She looked embarrassed and said that he had.

When I spoke about race tactics to Tommy Hoylake that Friday, he said not to worry, my father had rung him up and given him his instructions.

"And what were they?" I asked, with a great deal more restraint than I was feeling.

"Oh ... just to keep in touch with the field and not drop out of the back door when he blows up."

"Um. .... If he hadn't rung you up, how would you have planned to ride?" I said.

"Keep him well up all the time," he said promptly. "When he's fit, he's one of those horses who like to make the others try to catch him. I'd pick him up two furlongs out, take him to the front, and just pray he'd stay there."

"Ride him like that, then," I said. "I've got a hundred pounds on him, and I don't usually bet."

His mouth opened in astonishment. "But your father—"

"Promise you'll ride the horse to win," I said pleasantly, "or I'll put someone else up."

I was insulting him. No one ever suggested replacing Tommy Hoylake. He looked uncertainly at my open expression and came to the conclusion that because of my inexperience I didn't realize the enormity of what I'd said.

He shrugged. "All right. I'll give it a whirl. Though what your father will say . . ."

My father had not finished saying, not by six or more calls—mostly, it appeared, to the press. Three papers on the morning of the Lincoln quoted his opinion that Pease Pudding had no chance. He'd have me in before the Stewards, I grimly reflected, if the horse did any good.

Among all this telephonic activity, he rang me only once. Although the overpowering bossiness had not returned to his voice, he sounded stilted and displeased, and I gathered that the champagne truce had barely seen me out of the door.

He rang on the Thursday evening after I got back from Doncaster, and I told him how helpful everyone had been.

"Hmph," he said. "I'll ring the Clerk of the Course tomorrow, and ask him to keep an eye on things."

"Have you entirely cornered the telephone trolley?" I asked.

"Telephone trolley? Could never get hold of it for long enough. Too many people asking for it all the time. No, no. I told them I needed my own private extension, here in this room, and after a lot of fuss and delay they fixed one up. I insisted, of course, that I had a business to run."

"And you insisted often?"

"Of course," he said without humor, and I knew from

long experience that the hospital had had as much chance
as an egg under a steamroller.

"The horses aren't as backward as you think," I told
him. "You don't really need to be so pessimistic."

"You're no judge of a horse," he said dogmatically; and
it was the day after that that he talked to the press.

Major Barnette gloomed away in the parade ring and
poured scorn and pity on my hefty bet.

"Your father told me not to throw good money after
bad," he said. "And I can't think why I let you persuade
me to run."

"You can have fifty of my hundred, if you like." I offered it with the noblest of intentions, but he took it as a
sign that I wanted to get rid of some of my losses.

"Certainly not," he said resentfully.

He was a spare, elderly man of middle height, who
stood, at the slightest provocation, upon his dignity. Sign
of basic failure, I diagnosed uncharitably, and remembered the old adage that some owners were harder to train
than their horses.

The twenty-nine runners for the Lincoln were stalking
long-leggedly round the parade ring, with all the other
owners and trainers standing about in considering groups.
Strong, cold northwest winds had blown the clouds away,
and the sun shone brazenly from a brilliant high blue sky.
When the jockeys trickled through the crowd and emerged
in a sunburst into the parade ring, their glossy colors
gleamed and reflected the light like children's toys.

The old-young figure of Tommy Hoylake in bright
green bounced toward us with a carefree aura of play-it-
as-it-comes, which did nothing to persuade Major Barnette that his half share of the horse would run well.

"Look," he said heavily to Tommy, "just don't get
tailed off. If it looks as if you will be, pull up and jump
off, for God's sake, and pretend the horse is lame or the
saddle's slipped. Anything you like, but don't let it get
around that the horse is no good, or its stud value will
sink like a stone."

"I don't think he'll actually be tailed off, sir," Tommy
said judiciously, and cast an inquiring glance up at me.

"Just ride him as you suggested," I said, "and don't leave it all in the lap of the gods."

He grinned. Hopped on the horse. Flicked his cap to Major Barnette. Went on his lighthearted way.

The Major didn't want to watch the race with me, which suited me fine. My mouth felt dry. Suppose, after all, that my father was right, that I couldn't tell a fit horse from a letterbox, and that he in his hospital bed was a better judge. Fair enough; if the horse ran stinkingly badly, I would acknowledge my mistake and do a salutary spot of groveling.

Pease Pudding didn't run stinkingly badly.

The horses had cantered a straight mile away from the stands, circled, sorted, lined up, and started back at a flat gallop. I couldn't for a long time see Tommy at all, even though I knew vaguely where to look for him: drawn number twenty-one, almost mid-field. I watched the fast-moving mass making its distant way toward the stands, a multicolored charge dividing into two sections, one each side of the course. Each section narrowed until the center of the track was bare, and it looked as though two separate races were being held at the same time.

I heard his name on the commentary before I spotted the colors.

"And now on the stands' side it's Pease Pudding coming to take it up. With two furlongs to go, Pease Pudding on the rails with Gossamer next and Badger making up ground now behind them, and Willy Nilly on the far side followed by Thermometer, Student Unrest, Manganeta . . ." He rattled off a long string of names to which I didn't listen.

That he had been fit enough to hit the front two furlongs from home was all that mattered. I honestly didn't care from that moment whether he won or lost. But he did win. He won by a short head from Badger, holding his muzzle stubbornly in front when it looked impossible that he shouldn't be caught, with Tommy Hoylake moving rhythmically over the withers and getting out of him the last milligram of balance, of stamina, of utter bloody-minded refusal to be beaten.

In the winner's unsaddling enclosure, Major Barnette looked more stunned than stratospheric, but Tommy

Hoylake jumped down with the broadest of grins and said, "Hey, what about that, then? He had the goods in the parcel, after all."

"So he did," I said, and told the discountenanced pressmen that anyone could win the Lincoln any old day of the week: any old day, given the horse, the luck, the head lad, my father's stable routine, and the second-best jockey in the country.

About twenty people having suddenly developed a close friendship with Major Barnette, he drifted off, more or less at their suggestion, to the bar to lubricate their hoarse-from-cheering throats. He asked me lamely to join him, but as I had caught his eye just when, recovering from his surprise, he had been telling the world that he always knew Pease Pudding had it in him, I saved him embarrassment and declined.

When the crowd round the unsaddling enclosure had dispersed and the fuss had died away, I somehow found myself face to face with Alessandro, who had been driven to Doncaster that day, and the previous day, by a partially revitalized chauffeur.

His face was as white as his yellowish skin could get, and his black eyes were as deep as pits. He regarded me with a shaking, strung-up intensity, and seemed to have difficulty in actually saying what was hovering on the edge. I looked back at him without emotion of any sort, and waited.

"All right," he said jerkily, after a while. "All right. Why don't you say it? I expect you to say it."

"There's no need," I said neutrally. "And no point."

Some of the jangle drained out of his face. He swallowed with difficulty.

"I will say it for you, then," he said. "Pease Pudding would not have won if you had let me ride it."

"No, he wouldn't," I agreed.

"I could see," he said, still with a shake in his voice, "that I couldn't have ridden like that. I could see."

Humility was a torment for Alessandro.

I said, in some sort of compassion, "Tommy Hoylake has no more determination than you have, and no better hands. But what he does have is a marvelous judgment of pace and tremendous polish in a tight finish. Your turn will come, don't doubt it."

Even if his color didn't come back, the rest of the rigidity disappeared. He looked more dumfounded than anything else.

He said slowly, "I thought—I thought you would—what is it Miss Craig says?—rub my nose in it."

I smiled at the sound of the coloquialism in his careful accent.

"No, I wouldn't do that."

He took a deep breath and involuntarily stretched his arms out sidewise.

"I want—" he said, and didn't finish it.

You want the world, I thought. And I said, "Start on Wednesday."

When the horse box brought Pease Pudding back to Rowley Lodge that night, the whole stable turned out to greet him. Etty's face was puckered with a different emotion from worry, and she fussed over the returning warrior like a mother hen. The colt himself clattered stiff-legged down the ramp into the yard and modestly accepted the melon-sized grins and the earthy comments ("You did it, you old bugger") which were directed his way.

"Surely every winner doesn't get this sort of reception," I said to Etty after I'd come out of the house to investigate the bustle. I had reached the house half an hour before the horse, and found everything quiet; the lads had finished evening stables and gone round to the hostel for their tea.

"It's the first of the season," she said, her eyes shining in her good plain face. "And we didn't expect— Well, I mean—without Mr. Griffon and everything . . ."

"I told you to have more faith in yourself, Etty."

"It's bucked the lads up no end," she said, ducking the compliment. "Everyone was watching on TV. They made such a noise in the hostel they must have heard them at the Forbury Inn."

The lads were all spruced up for their Saturday evening out. When they'd seen Pease Pudding stowed safely away, they set off in a laughing and cheering bunch to make inroads into the stocks of the Golden Lion; and until I saw the explosive quality of their pleasure, I hadn't realized the extent of their depression. But they had after all, I reflected, read the papers. And they were used to believing my father rather than their own eyes.

"Mr. Griffon will be so pleased," Etty said, with genuine, unsophisticated certainty.

But Mr. Griffon, predictably, was not.

I drove down to see him the following afternoon and found several of the Sunday newspapers in the wastebasket. He greeted me with a face that made agate look like putty, and was watchfully determined that I shouldn't have a chance of crowing.

He needn't have worried. Nothing made for worse future relations in any field whatsoever than crowing over losers; and if I knew nothing else, I knew how to negotiate for the best long-term results.

I congratulated him on the win.

He didn't quite know how to deal with that, but at least it got him out of the embarrassment of having to admit he'd been made to look foolish.

"Tommy Hoylake rode a brilliant race," he stated, and ignored the fact that he had given him directly opposite instructions.

"Yes, he did," I agreed wholeheartedly, and repeated that all the rest of the credit lay with Etty and with his own stable routine, which we had faithfully followed.

He unbent a little, but I found, slightly to my dismay, that in contrast I admired Alessandro for the straightforwardness of his apology, and for the moral courage which had nerved him to offer it. Moral courage was not something I had ever associated with Alessandro before that moment.

Since my last visit, my father's room had taken on the appearance of an office. The regulation bedside locker had been replaced by a much larger table, which pushed around easily on huge wheel casters, like the bed. On the table was the telephone on which he had broadcast so much blight, also a heap of Racing Calendars, copies of the *Sporting Life,* entry forms, a copy of *Horses in Training,* the three previous years' form books, and, half hidden, the reports from Etty in her familiar schoolgirl handwriting.

"What, no typewriter?" I said flippantly, and he said

stiffly that he was arranging for a local girl to come in and take dictation sometime in the next week.

"Fine," I said encouragingly, but he refused to be friendly. He saw the winning of the Lincoln as a serious threat to his authority, and his manner said plainly that that authority was not passing to me, or even to Etty, while he could do anything to prevent it.

He was putting himself in a very ambivalent position. Every winner would be to him personally excruciating, yet at the same time he needed it desperately from the financial angle. Too much of his fortune for safety was still invested in half shares; and if the horses all ran as badly as it seemed he would like them to, their value would curl up like dahlias in a frost.

Understanding him was one thing, sorting him out quite another.

"I can't wait for you to get back," I said, but that didn't work either. It seemed that the bones were not mending as fast as had been hoped, and the reminder of the delay simply switched him into a different sort of aggravation.

"Some tommyrot about elderly bones taking longer to knit," he said irritably. "All these weeks, and they can't say when I can get out of all these comfounded pulleys. I told them I want a plaster cast I can walk on. Damn it, enough people have them, but they say there are lots of cases where it isn't possible, and that I'm one of them."

"You're lucky to have a leg at all," I pointed out. "At first they thought they would have to take it off."

"Better if they had." He snorted. "Then I would have been back at Rowley Lodge by now."

I had brought some more champagne, but he refused to drink any. Afraid it might look too much like a celebration, I supposed.

Gillie gave me an uncomplicated hug, and it was she who said, "I told you so."

"So you did," I agreed contentedly. "And, since I won two thousand pounds on your convictions, I'll take you to the Empress."

The tatty black, however, was tight.

"Just look," she wailed, pressing her abdomen with her

fingers, "I wore it only ten days ago and it was perfectly all right. And now it's impossible."

"I'm not overaddicted to flat-chested ladies with hip-bones sticking up like Mont Blancs," I said comfortingly.

"No, but voluptuous plenty can go too far."

"Grapefruit, then?"

She sighed, considered, went to fetch a cream trench coat which covered a multitude of bulges, and said cheerfully, "Whoever could do justice to Pease Pudding on a grapefruit?"

We toasted the victory in Château Figeac 1964 but, out of respect for the tatty-black seams, ate melon and steak and averted our eyes strong-mindedly from the puddings.

Gillie said over the coffee that owing to the continued shortage of orphans she was more or less having time off thrust upon her, and couldn't I think again and let her come to Newmarket.

"No," I said, more positively than I intended.

She looked a little hurt, which was unusual enough in her to bother me considerably.

"You remember those bruises I had, about five weeks ago?" I said.

"Yes, I do."

"Well, they were the beginning of a rather unpleasant argument I am still having with a man who has a strong line in threats. So far I have resisted some of the threats, and at present there's a sort of stalemate." I paused. "I don't want to upset that balance. I don't want to give him any levers. I've no wife, no children, and no near relatives except a father well protected in hospital. There's no one the enemy can threaten—no one for whose sake I will do anything he says. But, you see, if you came to Newmarket, there would be."

She looked at me for a long time, taking it in, but the hurt went away at once.

Finally, she said, "Archimedes said that if he could find somewhere to stand he could shift the world."

"Huh?"

"With a lever," she said, smiling. "You uneducated goose."

"Let's not give Archimedes a foothold."

"No." She sighed. "Set your tiny mind at rest. I'll pay you no visits until invited."

Back at the flat, lying side by side in bed and reading the Sunday papers in companionable quiet, she said, "You do see what follows from allowing him no levers?"

"What?"

"More bruises."

"Not if I can help it."

She rolled her head on the pillow and looked at me. "You know damn well. You're no great fool."

"It won't come to that," I said.

She turned back to the *Sunday Times*. "There's an advertisement here for travel on a cargo boat to Australia. Would you feel safer if I went on a cruise on a cargo boat to Australia? Would you like me to go?"

"Yes, I would," I said. "And no, I wouldn't."

"Just an offer."

"Declined."

She smiled. "Don't leave this address lying about, then."

"I haven't."

She put the paper down. "Just how much of a lever do you suppose I am?"

I threw the *Observer* onto the floor. "I'll show you, if you like."

"Please do," she said; and switched off the light.

chapter 12

"I would like you to come in my car to the races," I said to Alessandro on Wednesday morning when he turned up for the first lot. "Give Carlo a day off."

He looked back dubiously to where Carlo sat in the Mercedes, staring watchfully down the yard.

"He says I talk with you too much. He will object."

I shrugged. "All right," I said, and walked off to mount Cloud Cuckoo-land. We took the string down to Water-hall, where Alessandro rode a pipe-opener on Buckram and Lancat, and Etty grudgingly said that they both seemed to be going well for him. The thirty or so others that we took along didn't seem to be doing so badly, either, and the Lincoln booster was still fizzing around in grins and good humor. The whole stable, that week, had come alive.

Pulitzer had set off to Catterick early in the smaller of the stable's two horse boxes, accompanied by his own lad and the traveling head lad, Vic Young, who supervised the care of the horses while they were away from home. Second in command to Etty, he was a resourceful, quick-witted Londoner grown too heavy in middle age to ride most of the young stable inmates; but the weight came in useful for throwing around. Vic Young was a great one for getting his own way, and it was just good luck that his own way was usually to the stable's advantage. He was, like all the best older lads, deeply partisan.

When I went out after changing, ready to follow to the races, I found Alessandro waiting beside the Jensen, with Carlo glowering in the Mercedes six feet away.

"I will come in your car," announced Alessandro firmly. "But Carlo will follow us."

"Very well," I said, nodding.

I slid down into the driving seat and waited while he got in beside me. Then I started up, moved down the drive, and turned out of the gate with Carlo following in convoy.

"My father ordered him to drive me everywhere," Alessandro explained.

"And he doesn't care to disobey your father," I finished for him.

"That is right. My father also ordered him to make sure I am safe."

I slid a glance sidewise.

"Don't you feel safe?"

"No one would dare to hurt me," he said simply.

"It would depend what there was to gain," I said, speeding away from Newmarket.

"But my father . . ."

"I know," I said. "I know. And I have no wish to harm you. None at all."

Alessandro subsided, satisfied. But I reflected that levers could work both ways, and Enso, unlike me, did have someone for whose sake he could be forced to do things against his will.

Alessandro was impatient for the journey to be over, but was otherwise calmer than I had expected. Determination, however, shouted forth from the arrogant carriage of his head down to the slender hands which clenched and unclenched at intervals on his knees.

I avoided an oncoming oil tanker, whose driver seemed to think he was in France, and said casually, "You won't be able to threaten the other apprentices with reprisals if you don't get it all your own way. You understand that, don't you?"

He looked almost hurt. "I will not do that."

"The habits of a lifetime," I said without censure, "are apt to rear their ugly heads at moments of stress."

"I will ride to win," he asserted.

"Yes. . . . But do remember that if you win by pushing someone else out of the way, the Stewards will take the race away from you, and you'll gain nothing."

"I will be careful," he said, with his chin up.

"That's all that is required," I confirmed. "Generosity is not."

He looked at me with suspicion. "I do not always know if you are meaning to make jokes."

"Usually," I said.

We drove steadily north.

"Did it never occur to your father to buy you a Derby prospect, rather than to insert you into Rowley Lodge by force?" I inquired conversationally as we sped past Weatherby.

He looked as if the possibility were new to him. "No," he said. "It was Archangel I wanted to ride. The favorite. I want to win the Derby, and Archangel is the best. And all the money in Switzerland would not buy Archangel."

That was true, because the colt belonged to a great sportsman, an eighty-year-old merchant banker, whose lifelong ambition it had been to win the great race. His horses had, in years gone by, finished second and third, and he had won every other big race in the Calendar, but the ultimate peak had always eluded him. Archangel was the best he had ever had, and time was running short.

"Besides," Alessandro added, "my father would not spend the money if a threat would do instead."

As usual, when referring to his father's *modus operandi*, he took it entirely for granted and saw nothing in it but logic.

"Do you ever think objectively about your father?" I asked. "About how he achieves his ends, and about whether the ends themselves are of any merit?"

He looked puzzled. "No . . ." he said hesitantly.

"Where did you go to school, then?" I said, changing tack.

"I didn't go to school," he said. "I had two teachers at home. I did not want to go to school. I did not want to be ordered about and have to work all day."

"So your two teachers spent a lot of time twiddling their thumbs?"

"Twiddling—? Oh, yes. I suppose so. The English one used to go off and climb mountains and the Italian one liked the local girls." There was no humor in his voice. There never was. "They both left when I was fifteen. They left because I was then riding my two horses all day long, and my father said there was no point in paying for two tutors instead of one riding master, so he hired one old Frenchman who had been an instructor in the cavalry, and he showed me how to ride better. I used to go and stay with a man my father knew and go hunting on his horse and that is when I rode a bit in races. Four or five races. There were not many for amateurs. I liked it, but I didn't feel as I do now. . . . And then, one day at home when I was saying I was bored, my father said, 'Very well, Alessandro, say what you want and I will get it for you,' and into my head came Archangel, and I just said—just like that, without really thinking—'I want to win the English Derby on Archangel.' And he just laughed, how he sometimes does, and said, so I should." He paused. "After that, I asked him if he meant it, because the more I thought about it the more I knew there was nothing on the earth I wanted more. Nothing on the earth I wanted at all. He kept saying all in good time, but I was impatient to come to England and start, so when he had finished some business, we came."

For about the tenth time, he twisted round in his seat to look out the back window. Carlo was still there, faithfully following.

"Tomorrow," I said, "he can follow us again, to Liverpool. After Buckram for you tomorrow, we have four other horses running at the meeting, and I'm staying there for the three days. I won't be coming with you to Teesside for Lancat."

He opened his mouth to protest, but I said, "Vic Young is going up with Lancat. He will do all the technical part. It's the big race of the afternoon, as you know, and you'll be riding against very experienced jockeys. But all you've got to do is get quietly up on that colt, point it in the right direction, and tell it where to accelerate. And if it wins, for God's sake don't brag about how brilliant you are. There's nothing puts backs up quicker than a boastful jockey, and if you want the press on your side, which you most certainly do, you will give the credit to the horse. Even if you don't feel in the least modest, it will pay to act it."

He digested this thoughtfully.

I went on, "Don't despair if you make a right mess of any race. Everyone does, sometime. Just admit it to yourself. Never fool yourself, ever. Don't get upset by criticism. . . . And don't get swollen-headed from praise. . . . And keep your temper on a racecourse, all the time. You can lose it as much as you like on the way home."

After a while, he said, "You have given me more instructions on behavior than on how to win races."

"Well, you see, I trust your social manners less than your horsemanship."

He worked it out, and didn't know whether to be pleased or not.

After the glitter of Doncaster, Catterick Bridge racecourse disappointed him. His glance raked the simple stands, the modest weighing room, the small-meeting atmosphere, and he said bitterly, "Is this—all?"

"Never mind," I said, though I hadn't myself known what to expect. "Down there on the course are seven important furlongs, and they are all that matters."

The parade ring itself was attractive, with trees dotted all around. Alessandro came out in yellow and blue silks, one of a large bunch of apprentices, most of whom looked slightly smug or self-conscious or nervous, or all three at once.

Alessandro didn't. His face held no emotion whatsoever. I had expected him to be excited, but he wasn't. He watched Pulitzer plod round the parade ring as if it were of no more interest to him than a herd of cows. He settled into the saddle casually, and without haste gathered the reins to his satisfaction. Vic Young stood holding Pulitzer's rug and gazing up at Alessandro doubtfully.

"Jump him off, now," he said admonishingly. "You've got to keep him up there as long as you can."

Alessandro met my eyes over Vic's head. "Ride the way you've planned," I said, and he nodded.

He went away without fuss onto the course, and Vic Young, watching him go, exclaimed to me, "I never did like that snooty little sod, and now he doesn't look as though he's got his heart in the job."

"Let's wait and see," I said soothingly. And we waited. And we saw.

Alessandro rode the race exactly as he'd said he would. Drawn number five of sixteen runners, he made his way over to the rails in the first two furlongs, stayed steadfastly in fifth or sixth place for the next three, moved up slightly after that, and in the last sixty yards found an opening and some response from Pulitzer, and shot through the leading pair of apprentices not more than ten strides from the post. The colt won by a length and a half, beginning to waver.

He hadn't been backed and he wasn't much cheered, but Alessandro didn't seem to need it. He slid off the horse in the unsaddling enclosure and gave me a cool stare quite devoid of the arrogant self-satisfaction I had been expecting. Then, suddenly, his face dissolved into the smile I'd only seen him give that once to Margaret, a warm, confident, uncomplicated expression of delight.

"I did it," he said, and I said, "You did it beautifully," and he could certainly see that I was as pleased as he was.

Pulitzer's win was not popular with the lads. No one had had a penny on it, and when Vic got back and reported that the old horse must have developed a lot with age as Alessandro hadn't ridden to instructions, they were all quick to deny him any credit. As he seldom talked to any of them, however, I doubted whether he knew.

He was highly self-contained when he came to Rowley Lodge the following morning. Etty had gone down to the Flat on the racecourse side with the first lot to give them some longish steady canters, which, because of the distance I had to drive, I couldn't stay to watch. She seemed content to be left in charge for the three days, and had assured me that Lancat and Lucky Lindsay (bound for a two-year-old five furlongs with an experienced northern jockey) would arrive safely at Teesside on the Saturday.

Alessandro came to Aintree with me in the Jensen, with Carlo following as before. On the way, we mostly discussed the tactics he would need on Buckram and Lancat, and again there was an odd lack of excitement, only this time more marked. Where I would have expected him to be strung up and passionate, he was totally relaxed. Now that he was actually racing, it seemed as if his impatient fever had evaporated.

Buckram didn't win for him, but not because he didn't ride the race he had meant to. Buckram finished third because two other horses were faster, and Alessandro accepted it with surprising resignation.

"He did his best," he explained simply. "But we couldn't get there."

"I saw," I said; and that was that.

During the rest of the three-day meeting, I came to know a great many more racing people and began to get the feel of the industry. I saddled our other four runners, which Tommy Hoylake rode, and congratulated him when one of them won.

"Funny thing," he said. "The horses are as forward this year as I've ever known them."

"Is that good or bad?" I asked.

"Are you kidding? But the next trick will be to keep them going till September."

"My father will be back to do that," I assured him.

"Oh . . . yes. I suppose he will," Tommy said, without the enthusiasm I would have expected, and took himself off to weigh out for the next race.

On Saturday, Lancat cruised home by four lengths at Teesside at twenty-five-to-one, which increased my season's winnings from two thousand to four thousand five hundred. And that, I imagined, would be the last of the easy pickings; Lancat was the fourth winner from the stable out of eight runners, and no one was any longer going to suppose that Rowley Lodge was in the doldrums.

Alessandro's and Vic Young's accounts of what had happened at Teesside were predictably different.

Alessandro said, "You remember, in the trial, that I made up a lot of ground—but I did it too soon, because I had been left behind, and then he got tired. Well, he did produce that burst of speed again, just as we thought, and it worked well. I got him going a little before the last furlong pole and he simply zoomed past the others. It was terrific."

But Vic Young said, "He left it nearly too late. Got shut in. The others could ride rings round him, of course. That Lancat must be something special, winning in spite of being ridden by an apprentice having only his third race."

During the next week, we had eight more runners, of which Alessandro rode three. Only one of his was in an apprentice race, and none of them won. In one race, he was quite clearly outridden in a tight finish by the Champion Jockey, but all he said about that was that he would improve, he supposed, with practice.

The owners of all three horses turned up to watch, and raised not a grumble among them. Alessandro behaved toward them with sense and civility, though I gathered from an unguarded sneer he let loose when he thought no one was looking that he was acting away like crazy.

One of the owners was an American who turned out to be a subscriber to the syndicate which had bought out my antique shops. It amused him greatly to find I was Neville Griffon's son, and he spent some time in the parade ring before the race telling Alessandro that this young fellow here—meaning me—could teach everyone he knew a thing or two about how to run a business.

"Never forgot how you summed up your recipe for success when we bought you out. 'Put an eye-catcher in the window, and deal fair.' We'd asked you, remember? And we were expecting a whole dose of the usual management-school jargon, but that was all you said. Never forgot it."

It was his horse on which Alessandro lost by a head, but he had owned race horses for a long time and knew what he was seeing, and he turned to me in the stands immediately they had passed the post, and said, "Never a disgrace to be beaten by the champion. . . . And that boy of yours, he's going to be good."

The following week, Alessandro rode in four races and won two of them, both against apprentices. On the second occasion, he beat the previous season's star apprentice discovery on the home ground at Newmarket, and the press began to ask questions. Four wins in three weeks had put him high on the apprentice list. Where had he come from, they wanted to know. One or two of them spoke to Alessandro himself, and to my relief he answered them quietly. Strictly eyes down, even if tongue in cheek. The old habitual arrogance was kept firmly out of sight.

He usually came to the races in the Jensen, but Carlo never gave up following. The arrangement had become routine.

He talked quite a lot on the journeys. Talked naturally, un-self-consciously, without strain. Mostly we discussed the horses and their form and possibilities in relation to the opposition, but sometimes I had another glimpse or two of his extraordinary home life.

He had not seen his mother since he was about six, when she and his father had had a last appalling row which had seemed to him to go on for days. He said he had been frightened because they were both so violent, and he hadn't understood what it was all about. She kept shouting one word at his father, taunting him, he said, and he had remembered it, though for years he didn't know what it meant. Sterile, that had been the word. His father was sterile. He had had some sort of illness shortly after Alessandro's birth, to which his mother had constantly referred. He couldn't remember her features, only her voice beginning sentences to his father, bitterly and often, with "Since your illness . . ."

He had never asked his father about it, he added. It would be impossible to ask.

I reflected that if Alessandro was the only son Enso could ever have, it explained in some measure the obsessive side of his regard for him. Alessandro was special to Enso in a psychologically disturbing way, and Enso, with well-developed criminal characteristics, was not a normal character in the first place.

As Alessandro's riding successes became more than coincidences, Etty unbent to him a good deal; and Margaret unbent even more. For a period of about four days, there was an interval of peaceful, constructive teamwork in a friendly atmosphere. Something which, looking back to the day of his arrival, one would have said was as likely as snow in Singapore.

Four days, it lasted. Then he arrived one morning with a look of apprehension, and said that his father was coming to England. Was flying over that same afternoon. He had telephoned, and he hadn't sounded pleased.

chapter 13

ENSO MOVED into the Forbury Inn, and the very next day the prickles were back in Alessandro's manner. He refused to go to Epsom with me in the Jensen; he was going with Carlo.

"Very well," I said calmly, and had a distinct impression that he wanted to say something, to explain, to entreat—perhaps something like that—but that loyalty to his father was preventing it. I smiled a bit ruefully at him and added, "But any day you like, come with me."

There was a flicker in the black eyes, but he turned away without answering and walked off to where Carlo was waiting; and when we arrived at Epsom I found that Enso had traveled with him as well.

Enso was waiting for me outside the weighing room, a shortish chubby figure standing harmlessly in the April sunshine. No silenced pistol. No rubber-faced henchmen. No ropes round my wrists, needles in my arm. Yet my scalp contracted and the hairs on my legs rose on end. An indefinable quality of abnormality pervaded the atmosphere around him.

He held in his hand the letter I had written him, and the hostility in his puffy-lidded eyes beat anything Alessandro had ever conjured up by a good twenty lengths.

"You have disobeyed my instructions," he said, in the sort of voice which would have sent bolder men than I scurrying for shelter. "I told you that Alessandro was to replace Hoylake. I find that he has not done so. You have given my son only crumbs. You will change that."

"Alessandro," I said, with as unmoved an expression as I could manage, "has had more opportunities than most apprentices get in their first six months."

The eyes flashed with a thousand-kilowatt sizzle. "You will not talk to me in that tone. You will do as I say. Do you understand? I will not tolerate your continued disregard of my instructions."

I considered him. Where on the night he had abducted me he had been deliberate and cool, he was now fired by

some inner strong emotion. It made him no less dangerous. More, possibly.

"Alessandro is riding a very good horse in the Dean
Swift Handicap this afternoon," I said.

"He tells me this race is not important. It is the Great
Metropolitan which is important. He is to ride in that race
as well."

"Did he say he wanted to?" I asked curiously, because
our runner in the Great Met was the runaway Traffic, and
even Tommy Hoylake regarded the prospect without joy.

"Of course," Enso insisted, but I didn't wholly believe
him. I thought he had probably bullied Alessandro into
saying it.

"I'm afraid," I said with insincere regret, "that the
owner could not be persuaded. He insists that Hoylake
should ride. He is adamant."

Enso smoldered, but abandoned the lost cause. He said
instead, "You will try harder in future. Today I will over-
look. But there is to be no doubt, no shadow of doubt—
do you understand?—that Alessandro is to ride this horse
of yours in the Two Thousand Guineas. Next week he is
to ride Archangel, as he wishes. Archangel."

I said nothing. It was still as impossible for Alessandro
to be given the ride on Archangel as ever it was, even if I
wanted to, which I didn't. The merchant banker was
never going to agree to replacing Tommy Hoylake with an
apprentice of five weeks' experience, not on the starriest
Derby prospect he had ever owned. And for my father's
sake also, Archangel had to have the best jockey he could.
Enso took my continuing silence for acceptance, began to
look less angry and more satisfied, and finally turned his
back on me in dismissal.

Alessandro rode a bad race in the Handicap. He knew
the race was the Derby distance, and he knew I was giving him practice at the mile and a half because I hoped he
would win the big apprentice race of that length two days
later; but he hopelessly misjudged things, swung really
wide at Tattenham Corner, failed to balance his mount in
and out of the dip, and never produced the speed that was
there for the asking.

He wouldn't meet my eyes when he dismounted, and
after Tommy Hoylake won the Great Met (as much to

Traffic's surprise as to mine) I didn't see him for the rest of the day.

Alessandro rode four more races that week, and in none of them showed his former flair. He lost the apprentices' race at Epsom by a glaringly obvious piece of mistiming, letting the whole field slip him half a mile from home and failing to reach third place by a neck, though traveling faster than anything else at the finish.

At Sandown on the Saturday, the two owners he rode for both told me, after he trailed in mid-field on their fancied and expensive three-year-olds, that they did not agree that he was as good as I had made out, that my father would have known better, and that they would like a different jockey next time.

I relayed these remarks to Alessandro by sending into the changing room for him and speaking to him in the weighing room itself. I was now given little opportunity to talk to him anywhere else. He was wooden in the mornings and left the instant he dismounted, and at the races he was continuously flanked by Enso and Carlo, who accompanied him everywhere like guards.

He listened to me with desperation. He knew he had ridden badly, and made no attempt to justify himself. All he said, when I was finished, was "Can I ride Archangel in the Guineas?"

"No," I said.

"Please," he said with distress. "Please say I can ride him. I beg you."

I shook my head.

"You don't understand." It was an entreaty; but I wouldn't and couldn't give him what he wanted.

"If your father will give you anything you ask," I said slowly, "ask him to go back to Switzerland and leave you alone."

It was he then who shook his head, but helplessly, not in disagreement.

"Please," he said again, but without any hope in his voice, "I must—ride Archangel. My father believes that you are going to let me, even though I told him you wouldn't. . . . I am so afraid that if you don't, he really will destroy the stable—and then I will not be able to race again—and I can't—bear—" He limped to a stop.

"Tell him," I suggested without emphasis, "that if he destroys the stable you will hate him forever."

He looked at me numbly. "I think I would," he said.

"Then tell him so, before he does it."

"I'll—" He swallowed. "I'll try."

He didn't turn up to ride out the next morning, the first he had missed since his bump on the head. Etty suggested it was time some of the other apprentices had more chances than the very few I had given them, and indicated that their earlier ill feeling toward Alessandro had all returned with interest.

I agreed with her for the sake of peace, and drove off for my Sunday visit south.

My father was bearing the stable's successes with fortitude and finding some comfort in its losses. He did, however, seem genuinely to want Archangel to win the Guineas, and told me he had had long telephone talks with Tommy Hoylake about how it should be ridden.

He said that his assistant trainer was finally showing signs of coming out of his coma, though the doctors feared irreparable brain damage. He thought he would have to find a replacement.

His own leg also was mending properly at last, he said. He hoped to be home in time for the Derby; and he wouldn't be needing me after that.

The hours spent with Gillie were the usual oasis of peace and amusement, and bedtime was even more satisfactory than usual.

Most of the newspapers that day carried summings-up of the Guineas, with varying assessments of Archangel's chances. They all agreed that Hoylake's big-race temperament was a considerable asset.

I wondered if Enso read the English papers.

I hoped he didn't.

There were to be no race meetings for the next two days, not until Ascot and Catterick on Wednesday, followed by the Newmarket Guineas meeting on Thursday, Friday, and Saturday.

Monday morning, Alessandro appeared on leaden feet with charcoal shadows round his eyes, and said his father was practically raving because Tommy Hoylake was still down to ride Archangel.

"I told him," he said, "that you wouldn't let me ride him. I told him I understood why you wouldn't. I told him I would never forgive him if he did any more harm here. But he doesn't really listen. I don't know. . . . He's different, somehow. Not how he used to be."

But Enso, I imagined, was what he had always been. It was Alessandro himself who had changed.

I said merely, "Stop fretting over it and bend your mind to a couple of races you had better win for your own sake."

"What?" he said vaguely.

"Wake up, you silly nit. You're throwing away all you've worked so hard for. It soon won't matter a damn if you're warned off for life; you're riding so atrociously you won't get any rides anyway."

He blinked, and the old fury made a temporary comeback. "You will not speak to me like that."

"Want to bet?"

"Oh. . . ." he said in exasperation. "You and my father, you tear me apart."

"You'll have to choose your own life," I said matter-of-factly. "And if it still includes being a jockey, mind you win at Catterick. I'm running Buckram there in the apprentice race, and I should give one of the other lads the chance, but I'm putting you up again, and if you don't win they will likely lynch you."

He tried to lift his flagging spirits. His heart was no longer in it.

"And on Thursday, here at Newmarket, you can ride Lancat in the Heath Handicap. It's a straight mile, for three-year-olds only, and I reckon he should win it, on his Teesside form. So get cracking, study those races, and know approximately what the opposition might do. And you bloody well win them both. Understand?"

He gave me a long stare in which there was all of the old intensity but none of the old hostility.

"Yes," he said finally. "I understand. I am to bloody

well win them both." It was the first attempt at a joke I had ever heard him make.

Etty was rigidly angry over Buckram. My father would not approve, she said; and another private report was clearly on its way.

I sent Vic Young up to Catterick and went myself with three other horses to Ascot, telling myself that I was in duty bound to escort the owners at the bigger meeting, and that it had nothing to do with wanting to avoid Enso.

Out on the Heath, during the wait at the bottom of Side Hill for two other stables to complete their canters, I discussed with Alessandro the tactics he proposed using. Apart from the shadows which persisted round his eyes, he seemed to have regained some of his former race-day icy calm. It had yet to survive a long drive in his father's company, but it was a hopeful sign.

Buckram finished second. I felt distinctly disappointed when I saw his name on the "Results from Other Meetings" board at Ascot, but when I got back to Rowley Lodge Vic Young was just returning with Buckram, and he was, for him, enthusiastic.

"He rode a good race," he said, nodding. "Intelligent, you might say. Not his fault he got beat. Not like those stinking efforts last week. He didn't look the same boy, not at all."

The boy walked into the Newmarket parade ring the following afternoon with all the inward-looking self-possession I could want.

"It's a straight mile," I said. "Don't get tempted by the optical illusion that the winning post is much nearer than it really is. You'll know where you are by the furlong posts. Don't pick him up until you've passed the one with two on it, by the bushes, even if you think it looks wrong."

"I won't," he said seriously. And he didn't.

He rode a copybook race, cool, well paced, unflustered. From looking boxed-in two furlongs out, he suddenly sprinted through a split-second opening and reached the winning post an extended length ahead of his nearest rival. With his five-pound apprentice allowance and his Teesside form, he had carried a lot of public money, and he earned his cheers.

When he slid down from Lancat in the winner's unsaddling enclosure, he gave me again the warm rare smile, and I reckoned that, as well as too much weight and too much arrogance, he was going to kick the problem of too much father.

But his focus shifted to somewhere behind me, and the smile changed and disintegrated, first into a deprecating smirk and then into plain apprehension.

I turned round.

Enso stood inside the small white-railed enclosure.

Enso stared at me.

I had offered Alessandro a life of his own away from his father, set him on the way to success in the job he craved, and shown him that his father's values were not the only ones possible, and that others were saner.

To turn Alessandro gradually from a threat to an ally had been my solution to the problem. A quiet, productive outcome, because once Alessandro was totally committed to the stable, he would never allow his father to destroy it.

Alessandro was halfway across the bridge. And Enso guessed it. Enso was not going to allow me to take his son. Not if he could help it.

I stared back. Nothing else to do.

I was afraid.

I daresay it was asking for trouble to work at the desk in the oak room after I'd seen round the stables and poured myself a modest Scotch. But this time it was a fine light evening on the last day in April, not midnight in a freezing March.

The door opened with an aggressive crash and Enso walked through it with his two men behind him, the stony-faced familiar Carlo and another with a long nose, small mouth, and no evidence of loving-kindness.

Enso was accompanied by his gun, and the gun was accompanied by its silencer.

"Stand up," he said.

I slowly stood.

He waved the gun toward the door.

"Come," he said.

I didn't move.

The gun steadied on the central area of my chest. He

handled the wicked-looking thing as coolly, as familiarly, as a toothbrush.

"I am close to killing you," he said in such a way that I saw no reason not to believe him. "If you do not come at once, you will go nowhere."

This time, there were no little jokes about only killing people if they insisted. But I remembered; and I didn't insist. I moved out from behind the desk and walked woodenly toward the door.

Enso moved back to let me pass, too far away from me for me to jump him. But with the two now barefaced helpers at hand, I would have had no chance at all if I had tried.

Across the large central hall of Rowley Lodge, the main front door stood open. Outside, through the lobby and the farther doors, stood a Mercedes. Not Alessandro's. This one was maroon, and a size larger.

I was invited inside it. The American ex-rubber face drove. Enso sat on my right side in the back, and Carlo on the left. Enso held his gun in his right hand, balancing the silencer on his rounded knee, and his fingers never relaxed. I could feel the angry tension in all his muscles whenever the moving car swayed his weight against me.

The American drove the Mercedes northward along the Norwich road, but only for a short distance. Just past the Limekilns and before the bridge over the railway line, he swung off to the left into a small wood, and stopped as soon as the car was no longer in plain sight of the road.

He had stopped on one of the regular and often highly populated walking grounds. The only snag was that as all horses had to be off the Heath by four o'clock every afternoon, there was unlikely to be anyone at that hour along there to help.

"Out," Enso said, and I did as he said.

There was a short pause while the American, who seemed to be known as Cal to his friends, walked around to the back of the car and opened the boot. From it he took first a canvas grip, which he handed to Carlo. Next he produced a long darkish gray gabardine raincoat, which he put on although the weather was as good as the forecast. Finally he picked out with loving care a Lee Enfield .303.

Protruding from its underside was a magazine for ten bullets. He very deliberately worked the bolt to bring the first of them into the breech. Then he pulled back the short lever which locked the firing mechanism in the safety position.

I looked at the massive rifle which he handled so carefully yet with such accustomed precision. It was a gun to frighten with as much as to kill, though from what I knew of it, a bullet from it would blow a man to pieces at a hundred yards, would pierce the brick walls of an average house like butter, would penetrate fifteen feet into sand, and, if unimpeded, would carry accurately for five miles. Compared with a shotgun, which wasn't reliably lethal at a range of more than thirty yards, the Lee Enfield .303 was a dam-buster to a peashooter. Compared with the silenced pistol, which couldn't be counted on even as far as a shotgun, it gave making a dash for it over the Heath as much chance of success as a tortoise in the Olympics.

I raised my eyes from the source of these unprofitable thoughts and met the unwinking gaze of its owner. He was obscurely amused, enjoying the effect his pet had had on me. I had never, as far as I knew, met an assassin before; but without any doubt, I knew them.

"Walk along there," Enso said, pointing with his pistol up the walking ground. So I walked, thinking that a Lee Enfield made a lot of noise. The only thing was the bullet traveled one and a half times as fast as sound, so that you'd be dead before you heard the bang.

Cal had calmly put the big gun under the long raincoat and was carrying it upright with his hand through what was clearly a slit, not a pocket. From even a very short distance away, one would not have known he had it with him.

Not that there was anyone to see. My gloomiest assessments were quite right: we emerged from the little wood onto the narrow end of the Railway Field, and there wasn't a horse or a rider in sight.

Across the field, alongside the railway, there was a fence made of wooden posts with a wooden top rail and plain wire strands below. There were a few bushes bursting green round about, and a calm peaceful spring evening sunshine touching everything with red gold.

When we reached the fence, Enso said to stop.

I stopped.

"Fasten him up," he said to Carlo and Cal; and he himself stayed quietly pointing his pistol at me while Cal laid his deadly treasure flat on the ground and Carlo unzipped the canvas holdall.

From it he produced nothing more forbidding than two narrow leather belts, with buckles. He gave one of them to Cal, and without allowing me the slightest hope of escape, they turned my back toward the fence and each fastened one of my wrists to the top wooden rail.

It didn't seem much. It wasn't even uncomfortable; the rail was barely more than waist high. It just seemed professional, as I couldn't even turn my hands inside the straps, let alone slide them out.

They stepped away, behind Enso, and the sunlight threw my shadow on the ground in front of me. . . . Just a man leaning against a fence on an evening stroll.

Away in the distance on my left I could see the cars going over the railway bridge on the Norwich road, and farther still, down toward Newmarket on my right, there were glimpses of the traffic in and out of the town.

The town, the whole area, was bursting with thousands of visitors to the Guineas meeting. They might as well have been at the South Pole. From where I stood, there wasn't a soul within screaming distance.

Just Enso and Carlo and Cal.

I had watched Cal in his efforts on my right wrist, but it seemed to me shortly after they had finished that it was Carlo who had been rougher.

I turned my head and understood why I thought so. He had somehow turned my arm over the top of the rail and strapped it so that my palm was half facing backward. I could feel the strain taking shape right up through my shoulder and I thought at first he had done it by accident.

Then, with unwelcome clarity, I remembered what Dainsee had said: the easiest way to break a bone is to twist it, to put it under stress.

Oh, Christ, I thought; and my mind cringed.

chapter 14

I SAID, "I thought this sort of thing went out with the Middle Ages."

Enso was not in the mood for flippant comment.

Enso was stoking himself up into a proper fury.

"I hear everywhere today on the racecourse that Tommy Hoylake is going to win the Two Thousand Guineas on Archangel. Everywhere, Tommy Hoylake, Tommy Hoylake."

I said nothing.

"You will correct that. You will tell the newspapers that it is to be Alessandro. You will let Alessandro ride Archangel on Saturday."

Slowly I said, "Even if I wanted to, I could not put Alessandro on the horse. The owner will not have it."

"You must find a way," Enso said. "There is to be no more of this blocking of my orders, no more of these tactics of producing unsurmountable reasons why you are not able to do as I say. This time you will do it. This time you will work out how you *can* do it, not how you cannot."

I was silent.

Enso warmed to his subject.

"Also you will not entice my son away from me."

"I have not."

"Liar." The hatred flared up like magnesium, and his voice rose half an octave. "Everything Alessandro says is Neil Griffon this and Neil Griffon that and Neil Griffon says, and I have heard your name so much that I could *cut—your—throat!*" He was almost shouting as he bit out the last three words. His hands were shaking; and the gun barrel wavered round its target. I could feel the muscles tighten involuntarily in my stomach, and my wrists jumped uselessly against the straps.

He took a step nearer and his voice was loud and high.

"What my son wants, I will give him. *I . . . I . . .* will give him. I will give him what he wants."

"I see," I said, and reflected that comprehending the situation went no way at all toward getting me out of it.

"There is no one who does not do as I say," he

shouted. "No one. When Enso Rivera tells people to do things, they do them!"

Whatever I said was as likely to enrage as to calm him, so I said nothing at all. He took another step toward me, until I could see the glint of gold-capped back teeth and smell the sweet heavy scent of his after-shave.

"You, too," he said. "You, too, will do what I say! There is no one who can boast he disobeyed Enso Rivera. There is no one alive who has disobeyed Enso Rivera!" The pistol moved in his grasp and Cal picked up his Lee Enfield, and it was quite clear what had become of the disobedient.

"You would be dead now," he said. "And I want to kill you." He thrust his head forward on his short neck, the strong nose standing out like a beak and the black eyes as dangerous as napalm. "But my son—my son says he will hate me forever if I kill you. And for that I want to kill you more than I have ever wanted to kill anyone."

He took another step and rested the silencer against my thin wool sweater shirt, with my heart thumping away only a couple of inches below it. I was afraid he would risk it, afraid he would calculate that Alessandro would in time get over the loss of his racing career, afraid he would believe that things would somehow go back and be the same as on the day his son casually said, "I want to ride Archangel in the Derby."

I was afraid.

But Enso didn't pull the trigger. He said, as if the one followed inexorably from the other, as I suppose in a way it did, "So I will not kill you. . . . But I will make you do what I say. I cannot afford for you not to do what I say. I am going to make you."

I didn't ask how. Some questions are so silly they are better left unsaid. I could feel the sweat prickling out on my body, and I was sure he could read the apprehension on my face; and he had done nothing at all yet, nothing but threaten.

"Alessandro will ride Archangel," he said. "The day after tomorrow. In the Two Thousand Guineas."

His face was close enough for me to see the blackheads in the unhealthy putty skin.

I said nothing. He wasn't asking for a promise. He was telling me.

He took a pace backward and nodded his head at Carlo. Carlo picked up the holdall and produced from it a truncheon very like the one I had removed from him in Buckram's box.

Promazine first?

No promazine.

They didn't mess around making things easy, as they had for the horses. Carlo simply walked straight up to me, lifted his right arm with truncheon attached, and brought it down with as much force as he could manage. He seemed to be taking pride in his work. He concentrated on getting the direction just right. And it wasn't any of the fearsome things like my twisted elbow that he hit, but my collarbone.

Not too bad, I thought confusedly in the first two seconds of numbness, and anyway steeplechase jockeys broke their collarbones any bloody day of the week, and didn't make a fuss of it. But the difference between a racing fall and Carlo's effort lay in the torque and tension all the way up my arm. They acted like one of Archimedes' precious levers and pulled the ends of my collarbone apart. When sensation returned with ferocity, I could feel the tendons in my neck tighten into strings and stand out taut with the effort of keeping my mouth shut.

I saw on Enso's face a gray look of suffering—narrow eyes, clamped lips, anxious contracted muscles, lines showing along his forehead and round his eyes—and realized with extraordinary shock that what I saw on his face was a mirror of my own.

When his jaw relaxed a fraction, I knew it was because mine had. When his eyes opened a little and some of the over-all tension slackened, it was because the worst had passed with me.

It wasn't sympathy, though, on his part. Imagination, rather. He was putting himself in my place, to savor what he'd caused. Pity he couldn't do it more thoroughly. I'd break a bone for him any time he asked.

He nodded sharply several times, a message of satisfaction. There was still a heavy unabated anger in his manner and no guarantee that he had finished his evening's work. But he looked regretfully at the pistol, unscrewed the silencer, and handed both bits to Cal, who stowed them away under the raincoat.

Enso stepped close to me. Very close. He ran his finger down my cheek and rubbed the sweat from it against his thumb.

"Alessandro will ride Archangel in the Guineas," he said. "Because if he doesn't, I will break your other arm. Just like this."

I didn't say anything. Couldn't, really.

Carlo unfastened the strap from my right wrist and put it with the truncheon in the holdall, and they all three turned their backs on me and walked away across the field and through the wood to the waiting Mercedes.

It took a long inch-by-inch time to get my right hand round to my left, to undo the other strap. After that, I sat on the ground with my back against one of the posts to wait until things got better. They didn't seem to, much.

I looked at my watch. Eight o'clock. Time for dinner, down at the Forbury Inn. Enso probably had his fat knees under the table, tucking in with a good appetite.

In theory, it had seemed reasonable that the most conclusive way to defeat him had been to steal his son away. In practice, as I gingerly hugged to my chest my severely sore left arm, I doubted if Alessandro's soul was worth the trouble. Arrogant, treacherous, spoiled little bastard; but with guts and determination and talent. A mini battlefield, torn apart by loyalty to his father and the lure of success on his own. A pawn, pushed around in a power struggle. But this pawn was all, and whoever captured the pawn won the game.

I sighed, and slowly, wincing, got back on my feet. No one except me was going to get me home and bandaged up.

I walked. It was less than a mile. But far enough.

The elderly doctor was fortunately at home when I telephoned.

"What do you mean you feel off a horse and broke your collarbone?" he demanded. "At this hour? I thought all horses had to be off the Heath by four."

"Look," I said wearily, "I've broken my collarbone. Would you come and deal with it?"

"Mm," he grunted. "All right."

He came within half an hour, equipped with what looked like a couple of rubber quoits. Clavicle rings, he said as he proceeded to push one up each of my shoulders and tie them together behind my back.

"Bloody uncomfortable," I said.

"Well, if you will fall off horses . . ."

His heavy eyes assessed his handiwork with impassive professionalism. Tying up broken collarbones in Newmarket was as regular as dispensing cough drops.

"Take some codeine," he said. "Got any?"

"I don't know."

He clicked his tongue and produced a packet from his bag. "Two every four hours."

"Thank you. Very much."

"That's all right," he said, nodding. He shut his bag and flipped the clips.

"Have a drink?" I suggested as he helped me into my shirt.

"Thought you'd never ask," he said, smiling, and dealt with a large whiskey as familiarly as with his bandages. I kept him company, and the spirit helped the codeine along considerably.

"As a matter of interest," I said as he reached the second half of his glassful, "what illnesses cause sterility?"

"Eh?" He looked surprised, but answered straightforwardly, "Only two, really. Mumps and venereal disease. But mumps very rarely causes complete sterility. Usually affects one testicle only, if it affects any at all. Syphilis is the only sure sterility one. But with modern treatment, it doesn't progress that far."

"Would you tell me more about it?"

"Hypothetical?" he asked. "I mean, you don't think you yourself may be infected? Because if so—"

"Absolutely not," I interrupted. "Strictly hypothetical."

"Good." He drank efficiently. "Well. Sometimes people contract both syphilis and gonorrhea at once. Say they get treated and cured of gonorrhea, but the syphilis goes unsuspected. Right? Now, syphilis is a progressive disease, but it can lie quiet for years, doing its slow damage more or less unknown to its host. Sterility could occur a few years after infection. One couldn't say exactly how many years; it varies enormously. But before the sterility occurs, any number of infected children could be conceived. Mostly they are stillborn. Some live, but there's almost always something wrong with them."

Alessandro had said his father had been ill after he was born, which seemed to put him in the clear. But venereal disease would account for Enso's wife's extreme bitterness, and the violent breakup of the marriage.

"Henry the Eighth," the doctor said, as if it followed naturally on.

"What?" I said.

"Henry the Eighth," he repeated patiently. "He had syphilis. Catherine of Aragon had about a dozen stillborn children, and her one surviving child, Mary, was barren. His sickly son Edward died young. Don't know about Elizabeth, not enough data." He polished off the last drop of his glass.

I pointed to the bottle. "Would you mind helping yourself?"

He got to his feet and refilled my glass, too. "He went about blaming his poor wives for not producing sons, when it was his fault all the time. And that extreme fanaticism about having a son—and cutting off heads right and left to get one—that's typical obsessive syphilitic behavior."

"How do you mean?"

"The pepper king," he said, as if that explained all.

"What had he got to do with pepper, for heaven's sake?"

"Not Henry the Eighth," he said impatiently. "The pepper king was someone else. Look, in the medical textbooks, in the chapter on the advanced complications which can arise from syphilis, there's this bit about the pepper king. He was a chap who had megalomania in an interim stage of G.P.I., and he got this obsession about pepper. He set out to corner all the pepper in the world and make himself into a tycoon, and because of his compulsive fanaticism, he managed it."

I sorted my way through the maze. "Are you saying that at a further stage than sterility, our hypothetical syphilitic gent can convince himself that he can move mountains?"

"Not only convince himself," he agreed, nodding, "but actually do it. There is literally no one more likely to move mountains than your megalomaniac syphilitic. Not that it lasts forever, of course. Twenty years, perhaps, in that stage, once it's developed."

"And then what?"

"G.P.I." He took a hefty swallow. "General paralysis of the insane. In other words, descent to cabbage."

"Inevitable?"

"After this megalomania stage, yes. But not everyone who gets syphilis gets G.P.I., and not everyone who gets G.P.I. gets megalomania first. They're only branch lines—fairly rare complications."

"They would need to be," I said with feeling.

"Indeed, yes. If you meet a syphilitic megalomaniac, duck. Duck, quickly, because they can be dangerous. There's a theory that Hitler was one." He looked at me thoughtfully over the top of his glass, and his old damp eyes slowly widened. His gaze focused on the sling he had put round my arm, and he said as if he couldn't believe what he was thinking, "You didn't duck quick enough."

"A horse threw me," I said.

He shook his head. "It was a direct blow. I could see that—but I couldn't believe it. Thought it very puzzling, as a matter of fact."

"A horse threw me," I repeated.

He looked at me in awakening amusement. "If you say so," he said. "A horse threw you. I'll write that in my notes." He finished his drink and stood up. "Don't stand in his path any more, then. And I'm serious, young Neil. Just remember that Henry the Eighth chopped off a lot of heads."

"I'll remember," I said.

As if I could forget.

I rethought the horse-threw-me story and substituted a fall down the stairs for Etty's benefit.

"What a damn nuisance," she said in brisk sympathy, and obviously thought me clumsy. "I'll drive you along to Waterhall in the Land-Rover when we pull out."

I thanked her, and while we were waiting for the lads to lead the horses out of the boxes for the first lot, we walked round into bay one to check on Archangel. Checking on Archangel had become my most frequent occupation.

He was installed in the most secure of the high-security boxes, and since Enso's return to England I had had him guarded day and night. Etty thought my care excessive, but I had insisted.

By day, bay one was never left unattended. By night, the electric eye was positioned to trap unwanted visitors. Two specially engaged security men watched all the time, in shifts, from the owners' room, where the window looked out toward Archangel's box; and their Alsatian dog, on a long tethering chain, crouched on the ground outside the box and snarled at everyone who approached.

The lads had complained about the dog, because each time they had to see to any horse in bay one, they had to fetch the security guard to help them. All other stables, they had pointed out, had a dog on duty only at night.

Etty waved one arm to the guard in the window. He nodded, came out into the yard, and held his dog on a short leash so that we could walk by safely. Archangel came over to the door when I opened the top half, and poked his nose out into the soft Mayday morning. I rubbed his muzzle and patted his neck, admiring the gloss on his coat and thinking that he hadn't looked better in all the weeks I'd been there.

"Tomorrow," Etty said to him, with a gleam in her eyes, "we'll see what you can do, boy, tomorrow." She smiled at me in partnership, acknowledging finally that I had taken some share in getting him ready. During the past month, since the winners had begun mounting up, her air of constant worry had mostly disappeared, and the confidence I had remembered in her manner had all come back. "And we'll see how much more we'll have to do with him to win the Derby."

"My father will be back for that," I said, intending to reassure her. But the spontaneity went out of her smile, and she looked blank.

"So he will," she said. "Do you know . . . I'd forgotten."

She turned away from his box and walked out into the main yard. I thanked the large ex-policeman guard and begged him and his mate to be especially vigilant for the next thirty-four hours.

"Safe as the Bank of England, sir. Never you fear, sir." He was easy with certainty, but I thought him optimistic.

Alessandro didn't turn up to ride out, not for either lot. But when I climbed stiffly out of the Land-Rover after the second dose of Etty's jolting driving, he was standing waiting for me at the entrance to the yard. When I walked toward the door to the office, he came to meet me and stopped in my way.

I stopped also, and looked at him. He held himself rigidly, and his face was thin and white with strain.

"I am sorry," he said jerkily. "I am sorry. He told me what he had done. . . . I did not want it. I did not ask it."

"Good," I said casually. I thought about the way I was carrying my head on one side because it was less painful like that. I felt it was time to straighten up. I straightened.

"He said you would now agree to me riding Archangel tomorrow."

"And what do you think?" I asked.

He looked despairing, but he answered without doubt. "I think you will not."

"You've grown up a lot," I said.

"I have learned from you." He shut his mouth suddenly and shook his head. "I mean—I beg you to let me ride Archangel."

I said mildly, "No."

The words burst out of him, "But he will break your other arm. He said so, and he always does what he says. He'll break your arm again, and I—and I—" He swallowed and took a grip on his voice, and said with much more control, "I told him this morning that it is right that I do not ride Archangel. I told him that if he hurt you any more you would tell the Stewards about everything, and I would be warned off. I told him I do not want him to do any more. I want him to leave me here with you, and let me get on on my own."

I took a slow deep breath. "And what did he say to that?"

He seemed bewildered as well as distraught. "I think it made him even more angry."

I said in explanation, "He doesn't so much care about

whether or not you ride Archangel in the Guineas. He cares only about making me let you ride it. He cares about proving to you that he can give you everything you ask, just as he always has."

"But I ask him now to leave you alone. Leave me here. And he will not listen."

"You are asking him for the only thing he won't give you," I said.

"And what is that?"

"Freedom."

"I don't understand," he said.

"Because he did not want you to have freedom, he gave you everything else. Everything . . . to keep you with him. As he sees it, I have recently been holding out to you the one thing he doesn't want you to have. The power to make a success of life on your own. So his fight with me now is not really about who rides Archangel tomorrow, but about you."

He understood all right. And it was a revelation.

"I will tell him he has no fear of losing me," he said passionately. "Then he will do you no more harm."

"Don't you do that. His fear of losing you is all that's keeping me alive."

His mouth opened. He stared at me with the black eyes, a pawn lost between the rooks.

"Then what—what am I to do?"

"Tell him that Tommy Hoylake rides Archangel tomorrow."

His gaze wandered down from my face to the hump made by the clavicle rings and the outline of my arm in its sling inside my jersey.

"I cannot," he said.

I half smiled. "He will find out soon enough."

Alessandro shivered slightly. "You don't understand. I have seen. . . ." His voice trailed away and he looked back to my face with a sort of awakening on his own. "I have seen people he has hurt. Afterward, I've seen them. There was fear in their faces. And shame, too. I just thought—how clever he was—to know how to make people do what he wanted. I've seen how everyone fears him . . . and I thought he was marvelous." He took a shaky breath. "I don't want him to make you look like those others."

"He won't," I said, with more certainty than I felt.

"But he will not just let Tommy ride Archangel, and do nothing about it. I know him. . . . I know he will not. I know he means what he says. You don't know what he can be like. You must believe it. You must."

"I'll do my best," I said dryly, and Alessandro almost danced with frustration.

"Neil," he said, and it was the only time he had called me by my first name, "I am afraid for you."

"That makes two of us," I said. I looked at him with compassion. "Don't take it so hard, boy."

"But you don't—you don't understand."

"I do indeed understand," I said.

"But you don't seem to care."

"Oh, I care," I said truthfully. "I'm not mad keen on another smashing-up session with your father. But I'm even less keen on crawling along the ground to lick his boots. So Tommy rides Archangel, and we keep our fingers crossed."

He shook his head, intensely troubled. "I know him," he said. "I know him. . . ."

"Next week at Bath," I said, "you can ride Pulitzer in the apprentice race, and Clip Clop at Chester."

His expression said plainly that he doubted we would ever reach next week.

"Did you ever have any brothers or sisters?" I asked abruptly.

He looked bewildered at the unconnected question. "No. My mother had two more children after me, but they were both born dead."

chapter 15

SATURDAY MORNING, May 2nd. Two Thousand Guineas day.

The sun rose to another high golden journey over the Heath, and I inched myself uncomfortably out of bed with less fortitude than I would have admired. The thought that Enso could inflict still more damage was one I hastily shied away from; yet I myself had blocked all his tangents and left him with only one target to aim at. Having engineered the full frontal confrontation, so to speak, it was too late to wish I hadn't.

I sighed. Were eighty-five thoroughbreds, my father's livelihood, the stable's future, and perhaps Alessandro's liberation worth one broken collarbone?

Well, yes, they were.

But *two* broken collarbones?

God forbid.

Through the buzz of my electric razor I considered the pros and cons of the quick getaway. A well-organized, unfollowed retreat to the fastnesses of Hampstead. Simple enough to arrange. The trouble was sometime or other I would have to come back; and while I was away the stable would be too vulnerable.

Perhaps I could fill the house with guests and make sure I was never alone. But the guests would depart in a day or two, and Enso's idea of vengeance would be as strong as Napoleon brandy.

I struggled into a sweater and went down into the yard hoping that even Enso would see that revenge was useless if it lost you what you prized most on earth. If he harmed me any more, he would lose his son permanently. The only reasonable course now left to him was to retract his threats, salvage what he could of Alessandro's regard, and quietly go home.

But would he be—could he be—reasonable?

It had long been arranged that Tommy Hoylake should take the opportunity of his overnight stay in Newmarket to ride a training gallop in the morning. Accordingly, at seven o'clock he drove his Jaguar up the gravel and stopped outside the office window.

"Morning," he said, stepping out.

"Morning." I looked at him closely. "You don't look terribly well."

He made a face. "Had a stomach ache all night. Threw up my dinner, too. I get like that, sometimes. Nerves, I guess. Anyway, I'm a bit better now. And I'll be fine by this afternoon, don't worry about that."

"You're sure?" I asked with anxiety.

"Yeah." He gave a pale grin. "I'm sure. Like I told you, I get this upset now and again. Nothing to worry about. But look, would you mind if I don't ride this gallop this morning?"

"No," I said. "Of course not. I'd much rather you didn't. We don't want anything to stop you being all right for this afternoon."

"Tell you what, though. I could give Archangel his pipeopener. Nice and quiet. How about that?"

"If you're sure you're all right?" I said doubtfully.

"Yeah. Good enough for that. Honest."

"All right, then," I said, and he took Archangel out, accompanied by Clip Clop, and they cantered a brisk four furlongs, watched by hundreds of the thousands who would yell for him down on the racecourse that afternoon.

Etty was taking the rest of the string along to Waterhall, where several were due for a three-quarter-speed mile along the Line Gallop.

"Who shall we put on Lucky Lindsay, now we haven't got Tommy?" Etty said. And it presented a slight problem, because we were short of enough lads with good hands.

"I suppose we had better swap them around," I said, "and put Andy on Lucky Lindsay and Faddy on Irrigate, and—"

"No need," Etty interrupted, looking toward the drive. "Alex is good enough, isn't he?"

I turned round. Alessandro was walking down the yard, dressed for work. Long gone were the dandified clothes and the pale string gloves. He now appeared regularly in a camel-colored sweater with a blue shirt beneath, an outfit he had copied from Tommy Hoylake on the basis that if that was what a top jockey wore to ride out in, it was what Alessandro Rivera should wear, too.

There was no Mercedes waiting behind him in the drive. No watchful Carlo staring down the yard. Alessandro saw my involuntary search for the faithful attendant, and he said awkwardly, "I skipped out. They said not to come, but Carlo's gone off somewhere, so I thought I would. May I . . . I mean, will you let me ride out?"

"Why ever not?" said Etty, who didn't know why ever not.

"Go ahead," I agreed. "You can ride the gallop on Lucky Lindsay."

He was surprised. "But it said in all the papers that Tommy was riding that gallop this morning."

"He's got a stomach ache," I said, and, as I saw the wild hope leap in his face, added, "And don't get excited. He's better, and he will definitely be O.K. for this afternoon."

"Oh."

He smothered the shattered hope as best he could and went off to fetch Lucky Lindsay. Etty was riding Cloud Cuckoo-land, along with the string, but I had arranged to have George drive me down later in the Land-Rover in time to watch the gallops. The horses pulled out, circled in the paddock to sort out the riders, and went away out of the gate, turning left along the walking ground toward Waterhall.

With them went Lancat, but he, after his hard race two days earlier, was just to go as far as the main road crossing, and then turn back.

I watched them all go, glossy and elegant creatures on one of those hazy May mornings like the beginning of the world. I took a deep regretful breath. It was strange, but in spite of Enso and his son, I had enjoyed my spell as a race-horse trainer. I was going to be sorry when I had to leave. Sorrier than I had imagined. Odd, I thought. Very odd.

I walked back up the yard, talked for a few minutes to Archangel's security guard, who was taking the opportunity of his absence to go off to the canteen for his breakfast, went into the house, made some coffee, and took it into the office. Margaret didn't come on Saturdays. I drank some of the coffee and opened the morning mail by holding the envelopes between my knees and slitting them with a paper knife.

I heard a car on the gravel, and the slam of a door, and just missed seeing who was passing the window through misjudging the speed at which I could turn my head. Any number of people would be coming to visit the stable on Guineas morning. Any of the owners who were staying in Newmarket for the meeting. Anyone.

It was Enso who had come. Enso with his silenced leveler. He was waving it about, as usual. So early in the morning, I thought frivolously. Guns before breakfast. Damn silly.

The end of the road, I thought. The end of the damn bloody road.

If Enso had looked angry before, he now looked explosive. The short thick body moved like a tank round the desk toward where I sat, and I knew what Alessandro meant about not knowing what he could be like. Enso up in Railway Field had been an appetizer: this one was a holocaust.

He waded straight in with a fierce right jab onto the elderly doctor's best bandaging, which took away at one stroke my breath, my composure, and most of my resistance. I made a serious stab at him with the paper knife and got my wrist bashed against the edge of the filing cabinet in consequence. He was strong and energetic and frightening, and I was not being so much beaten by Enso as overwhelmed. He hit me on the side of my head with his pistol, and then swung it by the silencer and landed the butt viciously on my shoulder, and by that time I was half sick and almost past caring.

"Where is Alessandro?" he shouted, two centimeters from my right ear.

I sagged rather spinelessly against the desk. I had my eyes shut. I was doing my tiny best to deal with an amount of feeling that was practically beyond my control.

He shook me. Not nice. "Where is Alessandro?" he yelled.

"On a horse," I said weakly. Where else? "On a horse."

"You have abducted him," he yelled. "You will tell me

where he is! Tell me——or I'll break your bones. All of them."

"He's out riding a horse," I said.

"He's not!" Enso shouted. "I told him not to."

"Well . . . he is."

"What horse?"

"What does it matter?"

"What horse?" He was practically screaming in my ear.

"Lucky Lindsay," I said. As if it made any difference. I pushed myself upright in the chair and got my eyes open. Enso's face was only inches away, and the look in his eyes was a death warrant.

The gun came up. I waited numbly.

"Stop him," he said. "Get him back."

"I can't."

"You must. Get him back or I'll kill you."

"He's been gone twenty minutes."

"Get him back." His voice was hoarse, high-pitched, and terrified. It finally got through to me that his rage had turned into agony. The fury had become fear. The black eyes burned with some unimaginable torment.

"What have you done?" I said rigidly.

"Get him back," he repeated, as if shouting alone would achieve it. "Get him back!" He lifted the gun, but I don't think even he knew if he intended to shoot me or to hit me with it.

"I can't," I said flatly. "Whatever you do, I can't."

"He will be killed," he yelled wildly. "My son——my son will be killed!" He waved his arms wide and his whole body jerked uncontrollably. "Tommy Hoylake . . . It says in the newspapers that Tommy Hoylake is riding Lucky Lindsay this morning."

I shifted onto the front of the chair, tucked my legs underneath it, and made the cumbersome shift up onto my feet. Enso didn't try to shove me back. He was too preoccupied with the horror trotting through his mind.

"Tommy Hoylake . . . Hoylake is riding Lucky Lindsay."

"No," I said roughly. "Alessandro is."

"Tommy Hoylake. . . . Hoylake. . . . It has to be, it has to be!" His eyes were stretching wider and his voice rose higher and higher.

I lifted my hand and slapped him hard in the face.

His mouth stayed open, but the noise coming out of it stopped as suddenly as if it had been switched off.

Muscles in his cheeks twisted. His throat moved continuously. I gave him no time to get going again.

"You were planning to kill Tommy Hoylake."

No answer.

"How?" I said.

No answer. I slapped his face again, with everything I could manage. It wasn't very much.

"How?"

"Carlo . . . and Cal . . ." The words were barely distinguishable.

Horses on the Heath, I thought. Tommy Hoylake riding Lucky Lindsay. Carlo, who knew every horse in the yard, who watched all the horses every day and knew Lucky Lindsay by sight as infallibly as any tout. And Cal . . . I felt my gut contract much as Enso's must have done. Cal had the Lee Enfield .303.

"Where are they?" I said.

"I—don't—know."

"You'd better find them."

"They—are—hiding."

"Go and find them," I said. "Go out and find them. It's your only chance. It's Alessandro's only chance. Find them before they shoot him—you stupid, murdering sod."

He stumbled as if blind round the desk and made for the door. Still holding the pistol, he bashed into the frame and rocked on his feet. He righted himself, crashed down the short passage and out through the door into the yard, and half ran on unsure legs to his dark red Mercedes. He took three tries at starting the engine before it started. Then he swept round in a frantic arc, roared away up the drive, and turned right onto the Bury Road with a shriek of tires.

Bloody, murdering sod . . . I followed him out of the office but turned down the yard.

Couldn't run. The new hammering he'd given my shoulder made even walking a trial. Stupid, mad, murdering bastard. Twenty minutes since Alessandro rode out on Lucky Lindsay . . . twenty minutes, and the rest. They'd be pretty well along at Waterhall. Circling round at the end of the Line Gallop, forming up into groups. Setting off . . .

Damn it, I thought. Why don't I just go and sit down and wait for whatever happens. If Enso kills his precious son, serves him right.

I went faster down the yard. Through the gates into the bottom bays. Through the far gate. Across the little paddock. Out through the gate to the Heath. Turned left.

Just let him be coming back, I thought. Let him be coming back. Lancat, coming back from his walk, saddled and bridled and ready to go. He was there, coming toward me along the fence, led by one of the least proficient riders, sent back by Etty, as he was little use in the gallops.

"Help me take this jersey off," I said urgently to the rider.

He looked surprised, but lads my father had trained never argued. He helped me take off the jersey. He was no Florence Nightingale. I told him to take the sling off as well. No one could ride decently in a sling.

"Now give me a leg up."

He did that, too.

"O.K.," I said. "Go on in. I'll bring Lancat back later."

"Yes, sir," he said. And if I'd told him to stand on his head, he would have said "Yes, sir" just the same.

I turned Lancat back the way he had come. I made him trot along the walking ground. Breaking the Heath rules. Tut-tut. Breaking my own spirit, too. Cantering couldn't be worse. I twitched him out onto the Bury Hill ground which wasn't supposed to be used for another fortnight and pointed him straight at the Bury Road crossing.

Might as well gallop. . . . I did the first five furlongs on the gallop and the next three along the walking ground without slowing down much, and frightened a couple of early-morning motorists as I crossed the main road.

Too many horses on Waterhall. I couldn't from more than half a mile away distinguish the Rowley Lodge string from others. All I could see was that it wasn't yet too late. The morning scene was peaceful and orderly. No horrified groups bending over bleeding bodies.

I kept Lancat going. He'd had a hard race two days earlier and shouldn't have been asked for the effort I was urging him into. He was fast and willing, but I was running him into the ground.

It was technically difficult riding in clavicle rings, let alone anything else. However, the ground looked very hard and too far down. I stayed in the saddle as the lesser of two considerable evils. I did wish most fervently that I had stayed at home. I knew all about steeplechase jockeys riding races with broken collarbones. They were crazy. It was for the birds.

I could see Etty. See some of the familiar horses.

I could see Alessandro on Lucky Lindsay.

I was too far away to be heard even if I'd had any breath for shouting, and neither of them looked behind them.

Alessandro kicked Lucky Lindsay into a fast canter and, with two other horses, accelerated quickly up the Line Gallop.

A mile away, up the far end of it, there were trees and scrub and a small wood.

And Carlo. And Cal.

I had a frightful feeling of inevitable disaster, like trying to run away through treacle in a nightmare. Lancat couldn't possible catch the fresh Lucky Lindsay up the gallop. Interception was the only possibility, yet I could misjudge it so terribly easily.

I set off straight across Waterhall, galloping across the cantering ground and then charging over the Middle Canter in the opposite direction to the horses working there. Furious yells from all sides didn't deter me. I hoped Lancat had enough sense not to run head on into another horse, but apart from that my only worry—my sole, embracing, consuming worry—was to get to Alessandro before a bullet did.

Endless furlongs over the grass . . . only a mile, give or take a little . . . but endless. Lancat was tiring, finding every fresh stride a deeper effort. . . . His fluid rhythm had broken into bumps; he wouldn't be fit to race again for months. . . . I was asking him for the reserves, the furthest stores of power, and he poured them generously out.

Endless furlongs . . . and I wasn't getting the angle right. . . . Lancat was slowing and I'd reach the Line Gallop after Alessandro had gone past. I swerved more to the right ... swayed perilously in the saddle, couldn't even hold the reins in my left hand, and I wanted to hold on to the neck strap with my right, wanted to hold on for dear life, and if I held on, I couldn't steer ... It wasn't far, not really. No distance at all on a fresh horse. No distance at all for Lucky Lindsay.

All the trees and brushes up ahead. ... Somewhere in there lay Carlo and Cal ... and if Enso didn't know where, he wasn't going to find them. People didn't lie about in full sight, not with a Lee Enfield aimed at a galloping horse; and Cal would have to be lying down. Have to be, to be accurate enough. A Lee Enfield was as precise as any gun ever made, but only if one aimed and fired while lying down. It kicked too much to be reliable if one was standing up.

Enso wouldn't find them. He might find the car. Alessandro's Mercedes. But he wouldn't find Carlo and Cal until the thunderous noise gave away their position ... and no one but Enso would find them even then, before they reached the car and drove away. Everyone would be concentrating on Alessandro with a hole torn in his chest, Alessandro in his camel jersey and blue shirt which were just like Tommy Hoylake's.

Carlo and Cal knew Alessandro. ... They knew him well ... but they thought he had obeyed his father and stayed in the hotel ... and one jockey looked very like another from a distance, on a galloping horse. ...

Alessandro, I thought. Galloping along in the golden May morning ... straight to his death.

I couldn't go any faster. Lancat couldn't go any faster. Didn't know about the horse's breath, but mine was coming out in great gulps. Nearer to sobs, I daresay. I really should have stayed at home.

Shifted another notch to the right and kicked Lancat. Feeble kick. Didn't increase the speed.

We were closing. The angle came sharper suddenly as the Line Gallop began its sweep to the right. Lucky Lindsay came round the corner to the most vulnerable stretch. ... Carlo and Cal would be there. ... They would be ahead of him, because Cal would be sure of hitting a man coming straight toward him. There weren't the same problems as in trying to hit a crossing target.

They must be able to see me, too, I thought. But if Cal was looking down his sights, leveling the blade in the ring over Alessandro's tan sweater and bent black head, he wouldn't notice me ... wouldn't anyway see any significance in just another horse galloping across the Heath.

Lancat swerved of his own volition toward Lucky Lindsay and took up the race, a born and bred competitor determined even in exhaustion on getting his head in front.

Ten yards, ten feet ... and closing.

Alessandro was several lengths ahead of the two horses he had started out with. Several lengths ahead, all on his own.

Lancat reached Lucky Lindsay at an angle and threw up his head to avoid a collision, and Alessandro turned his face to me in wide astonishment; and although I had meant to tell him to jump off and lie flat on the ground until his father succeeded in finding Carlo and Cal, it didn't happen quite like that.

Lancat half rose up into the air and threw me, twisting, onto Lucky Lindsay, and I put my right arm out round Alessandro and scooped him off, and we fell like that down onto the grass. And Lancat fell, too, and lay across our feet, because brave, fast, determined Lancat wasn't going anywhere any more.

Half of Lancat's neck was torn away, and his blood and his life ran out onto the bright green turf.

Alessandro tried to twist out of my grasp and stand up.

"Lie still," I said fiercely. "Just do as I say, and lie still."

"I'm hurt," he said.

"Don't make me laugh."

"I have hurt my leg," he protested.

"You'll have a hole in your heart if you stand up."

"You are mad," he said.

"Look at Lancat. ... What do you think is wrong with him? Do you think he is lying there for fun?" I couldn't keep the bitterness out of my voice, and I didn't try. "Cal did that. Cal and his big bloody rifle. They came out here to shoot Tommy Hoylake, and you rode Lucky Lindsay instead, and they couldn't tell the difference, which should please you. . . . And if you stand up now they'll have another go."

He lay still. Speechless. And quite, quite still.

I rolled away from him and stuffed my fist against my teeth, for if the truth were told I was hurting far more than I would have believed possible. Him and his damn bloody father. . . . The free sharp ends of collarbone were carving new and unplanned routes for themselves through several protesting sets of tissue.

A fair amount of fuss was developing around us. When the ring of shocked spectators had grown solid and thick enough, I let him get up, but he only got as far as his knees beside Lancat, and there were smears of the horse's blood on his jodhpurs and jersey.

"Lancat," he said hopelessly, with a sort of death in his voice. He looked across at me as a couple of helpful onlookers hauled me to my feet, and the despair on his face was bottomless and total.

"Why?" he said. "Why did he do it?"

I didn't answer. Didn't need to. He already knew.

"I hate him," he said.

The people around us began to ask questions, but neither Alessandro nor I answered them.

From somewhere away to our right, there was another loud unmistakable crack. I and half the gathering crowd involuntarily ducked, but the bullet would already have reached us if it had been coming our way.

One crack, then silence. The echoes died quickly over Waterhall, but they shivered forever through Alessandro's life.

chapter 16

ENSO HAD found Carlo and Cal hidden in a clump of bushes near the Boy's Grave crossroads.

We found them there, too, when we walked along to the end of the Line Gallop to flag down a passing motorist to take Etty quickly into Newmarket. Etty, who had arrived frantic up the gallop, had at first, like all the other onlookers, taken it for granted that the shooting had been an accident. A stray bullet loosed off by someone being criminally careless with a gun.

I watched the doubt appear on her face when she realized that my transport had been Lancat and not the Land-Rover, but I just asked her matter-of-factly to buzz down to Newmarket and ring up the dead-horse removers, then to drive herself back. She sent Andy off with instructions to the rest of the string, and the first car that came along stopped to pick her up.

Alessandro walked off the training ground into the road with a stunned, stony face, and came toward me. He was leading Lucky Lindsay, which someone had caught, but as automatically as if he were unaware the horse was there. Three or four paces away, he stopped.

"What am I to do?" he said. He spoke without hope or anxiety. Lifeless. I didn't answer immediately, and it was then that we heard the voice.

A low distressed voice calling unintelligibly.

Startled, I walked along the road a little and through a thin belt of bushes, and there I found them.

Three of them. Enso and Carlo and Cal.

It was Cal who had called out. He was the only one capable of it. Carlo lay sprawled on his back, with his eyes open to the sun and a splash of drying scarlet trickling from a hole in his forehead.

Cal had a wider, wetter, spreading stain over the front of his shirt. His breath was shallow and quick; and calling out loud enough to be found had used up most of his energy.

The Lee Enfield lay across his legs. His hand moved

convulsively toward the butt, but he no longer had the strength to pick it up.

And Enso ... Cal had shot Enso with the Lee Enfield at a range of about six feet. It wasn't so much the bullet itself, but the shock wave of its velocity; at that short distance it had dug an entrance as large as a plate.

The force of it had flung Enso backward against a tree. He sat there now at the foot of it, with the silenced pistol still in his hand and his head sunk forward on his chest. There was a soul-sickening mess where his paunch had been, and his back was inseparable from the bark.

I would have stopped Alessandro seeing, but I didn't hear him come. I heard only the moan beside me, and I turned abruptly to see the sweat spring out on his face.

For Cal, Alessandro's appearance there was macabre.

"You ..." he said. "You ... are dead."

Alessandro merely stared at him, too shocked to understand, too shocked to speak.

Cal's eyes opened wide, and his voice grew stronger with a burst of futile anger.

"He said ... I had killed you. Killed his son. He was ... out of his senses. He said ... I should have known it was you. ..." He coughed, and frothy blood slid over his lower lip.

"You did shoot at Alessandro," I said. "But you hit a horse."

Cal said with visibly diminishing strength, "He shot Carlo ... and he shot me ... so I let him have it ... the son of a bitch. ... He was out ... of his senses. ..."

The voice stopped. There was nothing anyone could do for him, and presently, imperceptibly, he died.

He died where he had lain in wait for Tommy Hoylake. When I knelt beside him to feel his pulse, and lifted my head to look along the gallop, there in front of me was the view he had had: a clear sight of the advancing horses, through the sparse low branches of a concealing bush. The dark shape of Lancat lay like a hump on the grass three hundred yards away, and another batch of horses, uncaring, were sweeping round the far bend and turning toward me.

An easy shot, it had been, for a marksman. He hadn't bothered even with a telescopic sight. At that range, with a Lee Enfield, one didn't need one. One didn't need to be of pinpoint accuracy; anywhere on the head or trunk would do the trick. I sighed. If he had used a telescopic sight, he would probably have realized that what he was aiming at was Alessandro.

I stood up. Clumsily, painfully, wishing I hadn't got down.

Alessandro hadn't fainted. Hadn't been sick. The sweat had dried on his face, and he was looking steadfastly at his father.

When I moved toward him, he turned, but he needed two or three attempts before he could get his throat to work.

He managed it, finally. His voice was strained, different, hoarse; and what he said was as good an epitaph as any.

"He gave me everything," he said.

We went back to the road, where Alessandro had tethered Lucky Lindsay to a fence. The colt had his head down to the grass, undisturbed.

Neither of us said anything at all.

Etty clattered up in the Land-Rover, and I got her to turn it round and take me straight down to the town.

"I'll be right back," I said to Alessandro, but he stared silently at nothing with eyes that had seen too much.

When I went back, it was with the police. Etty stayed behind at Rowley Lodge to see to the stables, because it was still, and incredibly, Guineas day, and we had Archangel to look to. Also, in the town, I made a detour to the doctor, where I bypassed an outraged queue waiting in his surgery, and got him to put the ends of my collarbone back into alignment. After that, it was a bit more bearable, though nothing still to raise flags about.

I spent most of the morning up at the crossroads. Answered some questions and didn't answer others. Alessandro listened to me telling the highest up of the police who had arrived from Cambridge that Enso had appeared to me to be unbalanced.

The police surgeon was skeptical of a layman's opinion. "In what way?" he said without deference.

I paused to consider. "You could look for spirochetes," I said, and his eyes widened abruptly before he disappeared back into the bushes.

They were considerate to Alessandro. He sat on somebody's raincoat on the grass at the side of the road, and later on the police surgeon gave him a sedative.

It was an injection, and Alessandro didn't want it. They wouldn't pay attention to his objections, and when the needle went into his arm I found him staring fixedly at my face. He knew that I, too, was thinking about other injections; about myself, and Carlo, and Moonrock and Indigo and Buckram. Too many needles. Too much death.

The drug didn't put him out, just made him look even more dazed than before. The police decided he should go back to the Forbury Inn and sleep, and steered him toward one of their cars.

He stopped in front of me before he reached it, and gazed at me in awe from hollow dark sockets in a gray gaunt face.

"Look at the flowers," he said. "On the Boy's Grave."

When he had gone, I walked over to the raincoat where he had been sitting, close to the little mound.

There were pale yellow polyanthus, and blue forget-me-nots coming into flower round the edge; and all the center was filled with pansies. Dark dark purple velvet pansies, shining black in the sun.

It was cynical of me to wonder if he could have planted them himself.

Enso was in the mortuary and Alessandro was asleep when Archangel and Tommy Hoylake won the Guineas.

Not what the father and son had planned.

A heaviness like thunder persisted with me all afternoon, even though there was by then no reason for it. The defeat of Enso no longer directed half my actions, but I found it impossible in one bound to throw off his influence. It was not until then that I understood how intense it had become.

What I should have felt was relief that the stable was safe. What I did feel was depression.

The merchant banker, Archangel's owner, was practically incandescent with happiness. He glowed in the unsaddling enclosure and joked with the press in shaky pride.

"Well done, my boy, well done indeed," he said to me, to Tommy, and to Archangel impartially, and looked ready to embrace us all.

"And now, my boy, now for the Derby, eh?"

"Now for the Derby." I nodded, and wondered how soon my father would be back at Rowley Lodge.

I went to see him the next day.

He was looking even more forbidding than usual because he had heard all about the multiple murders on the gallops. He blamed me for letting anything like that happen. I saved him, I reflected sourly, from having to say anything nice about Archangel.

"You should never have taken on that apprentice."

"No," I said.

"The Jockey Club will be seriously displeased."

"Yes."

"The man must have been mad."

"Sort of."

"Absolutely mad to think he could get his son to ride Archangel by killing Tommy Hoylake."

I had had to tell the police something, and I had told them that. It had seemed enough.

"Obsessed," I agreed.

"Surely you must have noticed it before? Surely he gave some sign?"

"I suppose he did," I agreed neutrally.

"Then surely you should have been able to stop him."

"I did stop him—in a way."

"Not very efficiently," he complained.

"No," I said patiently, and thought that the only one who had stopped Enso efficiently and finally had been Cal.

"What's the matter with your arm?"

"Broke my collarbone," I said.

"Hard luck."

He looked down at his still-suspended leg, almost but not quite saying aloud that a collarbone was chicken feed compared with what he had endured. What was more, he was right.

"How soon will you be out?" I asked.

He answered in a smug satisfaction tinged with undisguisable malice. "Sooner than you'd like, perhaps."

"I couldn't wish you to stay here," I protested.

He looked faintly taken aback, faintly ashamed.

"No ... well ... they say not long now."

"The sooner the better," I said, and tried to mean it.

"Don't do any more work with Archangel. And I see from the Calendar that you have made entries on your own. I don't want you to do that. I am perfectly capable of deciding where my horses should run."

"As you say," I said mildly, and with surprisingly little pleasure realized that I now no longer had any reason for amending his plans.

"Tell Etty that she did very well with Archangel."

"I will," I said. "In fact, I have."

The corners of his mouth turned down. "Tell her that I said so."

"Yes," I said.

Nothing much, after all, had changed between us. He was still what I had run away from at sixteen, and it would take me a lot less time to leave him again. I couldn't possibly have stayed on as his assistant, even if he had asked me to.

"He gave me everything," Alessandro had said of his father. I would have said of mine that he gave me not very much. And I felt for him something that Alessandro had never through love or hate felt for his.

I felt ... apathy.

"Go away, now," he said. "And on your way out, find a nurse. I need a bedpan. They take half an hour, sometimes, if I ring the bell. And I want it now, at once."

The driver of the car I had hired in Newmarket was quite happy to include Hampstead in the itinerary.

"A couple of hours?" I suggested when I had hauled myself out onto the pavement outside the flat.

"Sure," he said. "Maybe there's somewhere open for tea, even on Sunday." He drove off hopefully, optimistic soul that he was.

Gillie said she had lost three pounds, she was painting the bathroom sludge green, and how did I propose to make love to her looked like a washed-out edition of a terminal consumptive.

"I don't," I said, "propose."

"Ah," she said wisely. "All men have their limits."

"And just change that description to looking like a race-horse trainer who has just won his first Classic."

She opened her mouth and obviously was not going to come across with the necessary compliment.

"O.K.," I said resignedly. "So it wasn't me. Everyone else, but not me, I do so agree. Wholeheartedly."

"Self-pity is disgusting," she said.

"Mm." I sat gingerly down in a blue armchair, put my head back, and shut my eyes. Didn't get much sympathy for that, either.

"So you collected the bruises," she observed.

"That's right."

"Silly old you."

"Yes."

"Do you want some tea?"

"No, thank you," I said politely. "No sympathy, no tea."

She laughed. "Brandy, then?"

"If you have some."

She had enough for the cares of the world to retreat apace: and she came across, in the end, with her own brand of fellow feeling.

"Don't wince when I kiss you," she said.

"Don't kiss so damned hard."

After a bit, she said, "Is this shoulder the lot? Or will there be more to come?"

"It's the lot," I said, and told her all that had happened. Edited, and flippantly; but more or less all.

"And does your own dear dad know all about this?"

"Heaven forbid," I said.

"But he will, won't he? When you get this Alessandro warned off? And then he will understand how much he owes you?"

"I don't want him to understand," I said. "He would loathe it."

"Charming fellow, your dad."

"He is what he is," I said.

"And was Enso what he was?"

I smiled lopsidedly. "Same principle, I suppose."

"You're a nut, Neil Griffon."

I couldn't dispute it.

"How long before he gets out of hospital?" she asked.

"I don't know. He hopes to be on his feet soon. Then a week or two for physiotherapy and walking practice with crutches, or whatever. He expects to be home before the Derby."

"What will you do then?"

"Don't know," I said. "But he'll be three weeks at least, and leverage no longer applies. . . . So would you still like to come to Rowley Lodge?"

"Mm," she said, considering. "There's a three-year-old Nigerian girl I'm supposed to be settling with a family in Dorset."

I felt very tired. "Never mind, then."

"I could come on Wednesday."

When I got back to Newmarket, I walked round the yard before I went indoors. It all lay peacefully in the soft light of sundown, the beginning of dusk. The bricks looked rosy and warm, the shrubs were out in flower, and behind the green-painted doors the six million quids' worth were safely chomping on their evening oats. Peace in all the bays, winners in many of the boxes, and an air of prosperity and timelessness over the whole.

I would be gone from there soon; and Enso had gone, and Alessandro. When my father came back, it would be as if these last months had never happened. He and Etty and Margaret would go on as they had been before; and I would read about the familiar horses in the newspapers.

I didn't yet know what I would do. Certainly I had grown to like my father's job, and maybe I could start a stable of my own, somewhere else. I wouldn't go back to antiques, and I knew by then that I wasn't going to work any more for Russell Arletti.

Build a new empire, Gillie had said.

Well, maybe I would.

I looked in at Archangel, now no longer guarded by men, dogs, and electronics. The big brown colt lifted his head from his manger and turned on me an inquiring eye.

I smiled at him involuntarily. He still showed the effects of his hard race the day before, but he was sturdy and sound, and there was a very good chance he would give the merchant banker his Derby.

I stifled a sigh and went indoors, and heard the telephone ringing in the office.

Owners often telephoned on Sunday evenings, but it wasn't an owner; it was the hospital.

"I'm very sorry," the voice said several times at the other end. "We've been trying to reach you for some hours now. Very sorry. Very sorry."

"But he *can't* be dead," I said stupidly. "He was all right when I left him. I was with him this afternoon, and he was all right."

"Just after you left," the voice said. "Within half an hour."

"But how?" My mind couldn't grasp it. "He only had a broken leg, and that had mended."

Would I like to talk to the doctor in charge? Yes, I would.

"He was all right when I left him," I protested. "In fact, he was yelling for a bedpan."

"Ah. Yes. Well," said a high-pitched voice loaded with professional sympathy. "That's—er—that's a very common preliminary to a pulmonary embolus. Calling for a bedpan—very typical. But do rest assured, Mr. Griffon, your father died very quickly. Within a few seconds. Yes, indeed."

"What," I said with a feeling of complete unreality, "is a pulmonary embolus?"

"Blood clot," he said promptly. "Unfortunately not uncommon in elderly people who have been bedridden for some time. And your father's fracture—well, it's tragic, tragic, but not uncommon, I'm afraid. Death sitting up, some people say. Very quick, Mr. Griffon. Very quick. There was nothing we could do, do believe me."

"I believe you."

But it was impossible, I thought. He couldn't be dead. I had been talking to him just that afternoon.

The hospital would like instructions, they delicately said.

I would send someone from Newmarket, I said vaguely. An undertaker from Newmarket, to fetch him home.

Monday I spent in endless chat. Talked to the police. Talked to the Jockey Club. Talked to a dozen or so owners who telephoned to ask what was going to happen to their horses.

Talked and talked.

Margaret dealt with the relentless pressure as calmly as she did with Susie and her friend. And Susie's friend, she said, had incidentally reported that Alessandro had not left his room since the police took him there on Saturday morning. He hadn't eaten anything, and he wouldn't talk to anyone except to tell them to go away. Susie's chum's mum said it was all very well, but Alessandro never had any money, and his bill had only been paid up to the previous Saturday, and they were thinking of asking him to go.

"Tell Susie's chum's mum that Alessandro has money here, and also that in Switzerland he will be rich."

"Will do," she said, and rang the Forbury Inn at once.

Etty took charge of both lots out at exercise, and somehow or other the right runners got dispatched to Bath. Vic Young went in charge of them and said later that the apprentice who had the ride on Pulitzer instead of Alessandro was no effing good.

To the police I told the whole of what had occurred on Saturday morning, but nothing of what had occurred before it. Enso had recently arrived in England, I said, and had developed this extraordinary fixation. There was no reason for them not to accept this abbreviated version, and nothing to be gained by telling them more.

Down at the Jockey Club, I had a lengthy session with a committee of members and a couple of Stewards left over on purpose from the Guineas meeting, and the outcome of what was equally peaceful.

After that, I told Margaret to let all inquiring owners know that I would be staying on at Rowley Lodge for the rest of the season, and they could leave or remove their horses as they wished.

"Are you really?" she said. "Are you staying?"

"Not much else to do, is there?" I said. But we were both smiling.

"Ever since you told that lie about not being able to find anyone to take over, when you had John Bredon lined up all the time, ever since then I've known you liked it here."

I didn't disillusion her.

"I'm glad you're staying," she said. "I suppose it's very disloyal to your father, as he only died yesterday, but I have much preferred working for you."

I was not so autocratic, that was all. She would have worked efficiently for anyone.

Before she left at three, she said that none of the owners who had so far telephoned were going to remove their horses; and that included Archangel's merchant banker.

When she had gone, I wrote to my solicitors in London and asked them to send back to me at Newmarket the package I had instructed them to open in case of my sudden death.

After that, I swallowed a couple of codeines and wondered how soon everything would stop aching, and from five to six-thirty I walked round at evening stables with Etty.

We passed by Lancat's empty box.

"Damn that Alex," Etty said, but with a retrospective anger. The past was past. Tomorrow's races were all that mattered. Tomorrow at Chester. She talked of plans ahead. She was contented, fulfilled, and busy. The transition from my father to me had been too gradual to need any sudden adjustment now.

I left her supervising as usual the evening feeds for the horses and walked back toward the house. Something made me look up along the drive, and there, motionless and only half visible against the tree trunks, stood Alessandro.

It was as if he had got halfway down the drive before his courage deserted him. I walked without haste out of the yard and went to meet him.

Strain had aged him so that he now looked nearer forty than eighteen. Bones stood out sharply under his skin, and there was little in the black eyes except no hope at all.

"I came," he started. "I need—I mean, you said, at the

beginning, that I could have half the money I earned racing. . . . Can I still—have it?"

"You can," I said. "Of course."

He swallowed. "I am sorry to come. I had to come. To
ask you about the money."

"You can have it now," I said. "Come along into the
office."

I half turned away from him but he didn't move.

"No. I . . . can't."

"I'll send it along to the Forbury Inn for you," I said.

He nodded. "Thank you."

"Do you have any plans?" I asked him.

The shadows in his face, if anything, deepened.

"No."

He visibly gathered every shred of resolution, clamped
his teeth together, and asked me the question which was
tearing him to shreds.

"When will I be warned off?"

Neil Griffon was a nut, as Gillie said.

"You won't be warned off," I told him. "I talked to the
Jockey Club this morning I told them that you shouldn't
lose your license, because your father had gone mad, and
they saw that point of view. You may not of course like it
that I stressed your father's insanity, but it was the best I
could do."

"But . . ." he said in bewilderment, and then in realiza-
tion, "Didn't you tell them about Moonrock and Indigo—and about your shoulder?"

"No."

"I don't understand . . . why you didn't."

"I don't see any point in revenging myself on you for
what your father did."

"But he only did it—in the beginning—because I
asked."

"Alessandro," I said. "Just how many fathers would do
as he did? How many fathers, if their sons said they wanted
to ride Archangel in the Derby, would go as far as murder
to achieve it?"

After a long pause, he said, "He was mad, then. He really was." It was clearly no comfort.

"He was ill," I said. "That illness he had after you were
born. It affected his brain."

"Then I—will not—?"

"No," I said. "You can't inherit it. You're as sane as anyone. As sane as you care to be."

"As I care to be," he repeated vaguely. His thoughts were turned inward. I didn't hurry him. I waited most patiently, because what he cared to be was the final throw in the game.

"I care to be a jockey," he said faintly. "To be a good one."

I took a breath. "You are free to ride races anywhere you like," I said. "Anywhere in the world."

He stared at me with a face from which all the arrogance had gone. He didn't look the same boy as the one who had come from Switzerland three months before, and in fact he wasn't. All his values had been turned upside down, and the world as he had known it had come to an end.

To defeat the father, I had changed the son. Changed him at first only as a solution to a problem, but later also because the emerging product was worth it. It seemed a waste, somehow, to let him go.

I said abruptly, "You can stay on at Rowley Lodge, if you like."

Something shattered somewhere inside him, like glass breaking. When he turned away, I could have sworn that against all probability there were tears in his eyes.

He took four paces, and stopped.

"Well?" I said.

He turned round. The tears had drained back into the ducts, as they do in the young.

"What as?" he said apprehensively, looking for snags.

"Stable jockey," I said. "Second to Tommy."

He walked six more paces away down the drive as if his ankles were springs.

"Come back," I called. "What about tomorrow?"

He looked over his shoulder.

"I'll be here to ride out."

Three more bouncing steps.

"You won't," I shouted. "You get a good sleep and a good breakfast and be here at eleven. We're flying over to Chester."

"Chester?" He turned as he shouted in surprise, and went two more steps, backward.

"Clip Clop," I yelled. "Ever heard of him?"

"Yes," he yelled back, and the laughter took him uncontrollably, and he turned and ran away down the drive, leaping into the air as if he were six.